I0535557

Perplexed

Teresa Lucas

Printed in the United States of America

10 9 8 7 6 5 4 3 2 1.

ISBN: 978-0-9907663-1-5
ISBN-10: 0990766314

Library of Congress Control Number: 2014920721

DEDICATIONS

To those I love and those who believe in me.

A special Thanks to

Ollie Harris and Stan Martin

For their continued belief in me.

ACKNOWLEDGMENTS

I like to acknowledge the people who have supported me so far. Your support has been my strength to keep writing. Instead of listing everyone names, I want to just say

Thank You

PERPLEXED

Chapter One

I had to look pass his broad shoulders to see the angry men blocking my doorway. I knew he would be pissed. Pissed about me leaving him. Leaving him to go live with another man. He hurt me. Hurt me in a way I never seen coming. Quentin. The men I have been in love with. Who I still love but I just need some time. Some time to figure out what I want and if what I have with Nathaniel is worth giving up Quentin.

Quentin and I were happy and I would have done anything for him. When he was kidnapped because of me and the bounty Rin had put out on Arashi and I, we went to go save him. We killed all of Rin's men and made it inside the dojo to save Quentin when we were attacked by someone much more powerful than us. It turned out the powerful person that was stronger than us was Quentin. He was working with Rin to capture and kill us. Rin had kidnapped Quentin's mother and told Quentin in order to get her back he had to kill me. I understood why he did what he did but it didn't stop me from feeling betrayed. It wasn't just that he tried to kill me; he has been lying and keeping who he really is from me. All this time he has been like me. We still haven't figured out who or what we are but we are different. We are stronger, faster and even more beautiful than normal people. We have ability's that we are still finding out about. Although I have never told Quentin about me, I have never shielded myself from him. Since he is like us, he has always been able to sense me. I could never sense him because he held himself back from me.

After seeing him today I just don't know if I'm ready to forgive and forget. After our argument earlier, I left in a hurry and came home to pack some things so that I can go back to Nathaniel place. I haven't known Nathaniel for a long time, but we have some type of connection that keep drawing us to each other. Nathaniel has been there for me every time I needed someone even when I didn't think I needed him. Now here he is again protecting me from the raging men blocking our exit.

Nathaniel moved in front of me to keep Quentin away from me. I know Quentin won't hurt me but Nathaniel is not taking any chances. The first time he met Quentin he was throwing him off me when he was just about to kill me. Nathaniel over powered Quentin and was about to kill him when I stopped him trying to explain the situation. Nathaniel didn't care why Quentin was willing to kill the women he is in love with. He figured with our abilities he should have made a different choice.

Quentin kept his gaze on Nathaniel, not underestimating him this time. They stood there for a long minute before someone actually spoke.

"Adena we're not finished talking about your decision." Quentin snapped at me without taking his eyes off Nathaniel.

"Quentin I made up my mind. Now move and let us go."

"You're not going to stay with another man without us figuring out things between us."

"There's nothing to figure out Quentin. I need time. You either going to give it to me or dislike the decision I make if I have to decide now." A shiver went down my back when Quentin took his gaze from Nathaniel to me. His eyes are cold and distant. They just stared at me and I saw the hurt in them. I knew that with Nathaniel standing here, Quentin wouldn't come to me. Quentin has always been a private person and there was no way he was going to talk about our relationship in front of Nathaniel. In a way this is good because his words won't be able to change my mind. I can stand strong about what I want and hopefully make it out the door without having to make a decision between Quentin and Nathaniel.

"Adena". Quentin says my name like he has just lost the only thing he ever cared about. I see his eyes soften and his body relax a little from holding all that tension. I wanted to go to him and tell him I'm sorry. Sorry for putting him in the position to have to kill me, and sorry for not being able to get over him trying to kill me. I opened my mouth to say something. Anything. But nothing came out so I closed my mouth and tried to control the emotion I know is showing in my eyes. As usual Quentin doesn't miss a beat. He has always been able to look at me and know what I am feeling.

Quentin noticed the struggle and emotion in my eyes. The private sorry I hide from him. He took a step forward and was short stopped by Nathaniel stepping completely in front of me blocking his view. I didn't have to see Quentin to know that he is pissed by Nathaniel protectiveness of me.

"I'm not going to hurt her." Quentin snapped at Nathaniel.

"I know". Nathanial said simply with a bit of humor in his tone.

Quentin and Nathaniel held each other gazes again. This time it seemed like forever. I finally opened my mouth to tell them to cut it out but stopped when Quentin turned his gaze to me and then back to Nathaniel.

"I won't give up Adena". Quentin said while holding Nathaniel gaze. I thought he was telling Nathaniel until he turned his gaze back to me. "I will win you back". Quentin held my gaze a few seconds more and finally stepped to the side to let us pass.

I woke up this morning still feeling a little sad but I am determined to get up and ready to start living what little of a normal life I have left. First thing on my list to do is jump back into action with work. I've been gone a while and my clients are starting to get worried. It's time to go into the office and show them just why I am the best at what I do.

Nathaniel gives me some much needed space after last night run in with Quentin. When I get ready to leave for work I give Nathaniel an awkward kiss and tell him I'll see him later.

The good thing about staying with Nathaniel is that he already stays downtown. It's a nice walk to work when the weather is good. We all know the windy city weather can go either way. Since it's the middle of June, the weather is pretty good but I decided to take a cab to work so I won't distract myself with the view of all the stores on Michigan Ave.

"Hi Ms. Hartworth. It's nice to have you back." Gia says as I walk through my office door. Gia is my personal assistant. She's been working for me for the past four years now. She's great at what she do because there is nothing she can't do. She doesn't back down to anyone including me. Gia always has a bubbly attitude that always helps brighten my day in the morning. She is 5'6, slim, light caramel skin tone, has long brown hair, and green eyes. She's a very beautiful women and she knows it. At the age of 25 she is doing very well for herself.

"Hi Gia. Any messages?" I ask knowing the depth of just how many messages I have waiting for me.

"That's a joke right? You lucky I like my job or I'll be kicking your ass right now". Gia snaps. It feels good being back already and seeing that Gia hasn't changed while I was gone.

"Yea, yea, yea. Just update me already." I said and continue my slow pace into my office while Gia talk away.

My first day ends in success. I was able to communicate with my clients to ensure them their best interest is always at the forefront of my mind and catch up on some much needed research. I need to stay ahead of my competitors and make sure my clients always profit from my choices.

I decided to stay at work longer than usual and I am now feeling the exhaustion of making phone calls and staring at a computer screen all day. All I want to do now is crawl into bed and go to sleep. I sent Gia home at five. There was no need for her to stay and suffer for my need to catch up. Finally, I lock up and hail a cab to Nathaniel place.

It is hard to keep my eyes open on the ride home. I don't remember much of the ride just that the cab man announce we made it. I pay him and head up to Nathaniel's place. I'm hoping to go straight to bed but Nathaniel is waiting for me.

"Welcome home beautiful".

"Thank you". I respond as I take in the scenery. Nathaniel dimmed the lights, lit some candles and cooked what smells like a delicious dinner. "What is all this for?"

"Your first day back to work had to be long so I wanted you to come home and relax." Nathaniel says as he walk towards me holding two wine glasses in his hand.

I want to say thank you. Thank you for being so thoughtful but all I want to do is go to sleep. But I don't. I take the wine glass he hands me and drink it down. I'm going to need it if I'm going to have to stay up.

"Thank you". I hand Nathaniel the empty wine glass and watch as he put the glasses on the table. When he's done he turns his attention back to me and slowly takes his eyes up my body and stop when he reaches my breast. I can't help it. My breathing gets heavier and my body starts to respond to his intense sexual gaze over my breast. I try controlling my breathing but end up settling for just holding my breath. I can't believe my body is responding so erotically to his gaze while my mind is fighting to stay awake.

I watch Nathaniel as he start a slow glide towards me. Or should I say my breast since his gaze is still locked on them and my nipples as they start to harden with each step he takes. He finally stops right in front of me and bring his eyes to look into mine. I stand still, still holding my breath waiting to see what he will do next. He holds may gaze and suddenly I gasp, finally taking in air from his sudden pinch of my nipple. My body is instantly aroused while my mind gets instantly pissed from the sudden feelings keeping me from the sleep I desperately need.

"Your first day must have been longer then you anticipated it to be. Did you even see Arashi today?" Nathaniel asked while he continued to torture my nipple.

"No I did not see Arashi today." I say as I try to control the mixed feelings of arousal and anger emerging at the same time.

"Let's see if I can relax you a little." Nathaniel says to me with a low seductive smile on his face.

"Is this why you wanted me to stay with you? So you can have your way with me whenever you want." I respond with a little bit more attitude then I expected.

"One of the reasons." Nathaniel says right before he spread my legs, put his hand up my skirt, moves my panties to the side, and starts moving his thumb in a fast circular motion on my clitoris. "Is there a problem Adena? Do you want me to stop?"

I barely hear his questions over the load moaning and hypnotic gyrating of my body that I am apparently doing. But I manage to answer still holding on to the little anger I have left. "Yes."

"Then tell me to stop." Nathaniel says as his thumb start to move faster and harder on my clitoris. I feel my orgasm rising. I'm on the edge of releasing when Nathaniel suddenly stops.

"NO!" I scream. Why did you stop?" I ask pissed because I was ready to cum. I need to cum now that he brought me to the edge.

"You wanted me to stop. Let's go eat before the food gets cold." Nathaniel walks over to the table he set up and pulls out the chair for me to sit. I am so pissed and in heat right now that all I can do is think about the different ways to kick Nathaniel's ass. I just stand here watching him. I refuse to move until he turn and look over at me. He looks me up and down and raise's his eyebrow at me and then smile before stepping to the side to hold his hand out to me.

It just pisses me off more. He knows he is torturing me and that I am mad ass hell.

I take a deep breath and walk towards the table. Instead of stopping and sitting down, I walk past Nathaniel and go straight to his room. I am too pissed to sit across a table from him and play whatever game he's playing.

I know I won't be able to go to sleep but I lay down anyway. I focus on controlling my breathing and counting to ten at least thirty times. It must have worked because I drifted off to sleep. I don't stay sleep long before I am overloaded with the feeling to cum. The feeling is so intense I arched my back and push my head into the bed as far as the mattress would let me. My hands find Nathaniel's head between my legs as his tongue work his way in and out of my pussy. I can't help the need to lift my pussy into his face as if I want him to swallow me whole. He moves his tongue in and out of my pussy hitting spots I didn't even know I had. He moves his tongue to my clitoris and gives it one slow, long, hard lick and I start shivering. One more lick and I would explode harder than I ever have but the lick never came.

"Nathaniel Please." I plead. I can't wait any longer. I need to cum now. Right now. I didn't feel Nathaniel between my legs anymore. I reach for him and only grasped air. I'm about to open my eyes when I feel Nathaniel dick pressing against the opening of my pussy. I lift myself up trying to push him inside me but Nathaniel pushes me back down and holds me in place against the mattress. "Please Nathaniel." I plead again.

He slowly pushes his dick inside me. The growl that escapes from me is loud and unexpected. I want him to pound into me and fuck me until I explode in orgasm, but Nathaniel begin a slow grind. The grind is deep and mind blowing. I try lifting my hips again to get him to speed up but Nathaniel grip is too tight. I have no choice but to take the slow grind he gives me. It continues at this pace for the next few minutes. It feels like forever and I need more. I grip both his wrist that is pining me down and start to aggressively move against him to increase the speed. Nathaniel grip only gets stronger and I start to feel the pain from his grip on my waist.

I can't take it no more so I start to hit Nathaniel. I don't care anymore. I want him to either fuck me or get out of me. The only thing I can reach is his arms. I start to hit his arms so I can finally get up but then Nathaniel crashes into me. He starts to fuck me hard and fast and my orgasm starts to build up again.

"Yes. Keep going. I'm almost there." I moan. I'm ready to explode. Ready to cum, I throw my head back and I am about to release my orgasm when Nathaniel pulls out of me suddenly.

"NO! I hate you. Get off me. Get off me now." I snap.

"You want to tell me why I prepared you a nice dinner and you're in here sleep instead of out there eating with me?" Nathaniel snapped back.

"Screw you."

"That's exactly what you're doing." Nathaniel replied as he started his slow grind into me again.

"I don't want you in me. Get out of me Nathaniel. I mean it."

"NO! I'm going to stay in you until you tell me what's wrong with you."

"You're what's wrong with me."

"You came in the door mad. Did something happen at work and you decided to come home and take it out on me?"

"No."

"Then what Adena?" Nathaniel asks as he crash into me again.

"AH! Nathaniel please." I plead again. "I can't take no more."

"Then tell me what's wrong with you."

"Nothing."

"Adena." He snaps through clinch teeth and slams into me again.

"AH!"

"Tell me or I'm pulling out again."

"No. I was tired when I got off and all I wanted to do was sleep but when I came in you had already had all this planned and I didn't want to seem ungrateful but I was getting angrier every minute I forced myself to stay woke." I babbled out fast hoping Nathaniel would let me cum or leave me alone.

"You should have just said that."

"Please Nathaniel." I plead again. Nathaniel finally starts to move fast and hard and my orgasm quickly starts to rise again. I don't know if Nathaniel will let me cum but I feel the tears running down my cheeks.

"Cum baby. Cum for me." Nathaniel says and I explode. It is the most intense orgasm I have ever had. I start coming down from my orgasm when Nathaniel began to stroke my clitoris. It doesn't take much and I explode again. I feel Nathaniel as he continues to push in and out of me faster and faster until he finally explode. His orgasm is long and the growl he makes during his orgasm is loud, long, and desperate. He collapses on the side of me. I'm too weak to even turn to him.

Nathaniel turns me to my side and pulls me into him. I can feel myself drifting to sleep when Nathaniel put one of his legs between mine and use his fingers to rub my clitoris again.

"Nathaniel no. I can't take no more. NO!" I scream as I bucked and try to move away from Nathaniel torturing.

"It's okay baby. I got you. Just let it come."

I'm about to protest again when another orgasm explodes from me again. Everything goes black and I'm out cold.

Chapter Two

I wake up this morning feeling thoroughly fucked. I'm not sure if I can even move. I test my joints and as I expected I am extremely sore. I have no I idea how I'm going to get through a full day of work like this. HOLY SHIT! WORK! I'm going to be late. I look around for the clock and find it on the bedside table. I have less than thirty minutes to make it to work. I jump out of bed as fast as I can considering how much pain I am in. I make it to the bathroom and rush in the shower. I somehow manage to get done with everything in fifteen minutes. I grab my things and head out the door running into Nathaniel with a smile from ear to ear on his face.

"Don't look at me like that. Why didn't you wake me?"

"I didn't think you would be up for going to work when you got up this morning."

"I have to go to work. It's only my second day back."

"You can work from home Adena. You own the company."

"I like working in my office. I don't have time to talk about this now I have to go." I wave bye to Nathaniel on my way out the door. That man is going to drive me crazy one day.

I make it to work at exactly nine and hate that I have this just fucked walk again. It's embarrassing but I refuse to miss a day of work because I was overly fucked. Not exactly the best reason to give my clients.

"Ms. Hartworth welcome to day two of your work week." Gia says when I walk into the office.

"Would you stop calling me that? Call me Adena."

"Just trying to keep it professional around here".

"Since when?"

"Hey, a lot of things have changed since you took your extended vacation. I'm embracing my professional side."

"You should have done that when I hired you. So stop calling me that or you're fired."

"Ha ha ha. No one knows you better than me in this office. I made it damn hard for you to replace me over what name I call you."

"You getting a little cocky aren't you?"

"No. I always been cocky and I know my worth."

"What did I get myself into?" I say as I walk pass Gia and head to my office.

"I don't know, but it must have been good judging from that walk."

"What happen to embracing your professional side?"

"Honey that only extended to your name. Now give me the dirt. Quentin must have hit it real good last night for you to be walking into work like that."

"No Quentin didn't and we are not talking about this." I try to avoid the uncomfortable conversation about Quentin and Nathaniel. There is no way for me to tell her how Nathaniel and I met without mentioning who or what we are. I still don't know the answer to that myself.

"Oh, you're not getting out of this that easy. If it wasn't Quentin, then who put that walk on you? Somebody did. Who was it? Better yet why wasn't it Quentin?"

"We broke up."

"When? And you bounced back already. This new guy must really be good in the sack because I thought Quentin was it for you."

"I did to. It's a long story that I don't feel like talking about right now. Do I have any messages?"

"Yes. Mr. Fairchild called in. He has some questions about a new company he's looking to invest in and want you to call him when you have time to talk."

"Did he say what company?"

"Yes. A company called Techsmart."

"Okay. Get me all the information you can on the company, the owner and make sure to find out there financial information. Especially who is doing there financing and what bank they're working with. I want to make a few investigative calls before I call Fairchild back."

"I'll get right on it."

Gia left my office to start researching the company and I decided to make some calls to some associates I have in the tech world to see if they know anything about this up and coming company. Mr. Fairchild usually make good decision but I like to make sure the company is worth the risk and if it is, I find multiple ways to profit from the company on both my client and my behalf.

I finally finish making calls to my associates and decide to do some light research on the internet. I'm deep into work mood when Gia voice come through my desk phone and makes me jump.

"There's a Mr. Stock here to see you."

Nathaniel. What is he doing here? Something must have happened for him to be at my office. I rush to my office door and suddenly stop to take in the gorgeous view of Nathaniel. He has on a Dark grey suit with a slick black tie on top of a well fitted white dress shirt. It looks as if it was tailored made to his body and boy does his body look good in that suit. My gaze travels down his body and land on the black square toes he have on that compliments the suit perfection. When my gaze finally makes it back to Nathaniel's face he is staring at me with a small smile on his face.

"Am I disturbing you?"

"Not at all. Is something wrong?"

"No. I wanted to know if you have time to have lunch with me."

"Dinner last night wasn't enough?" I say raising one eyebrow up to him since we didn't eat dinner last night. I notice Nathaniel smile widen and he starts a slow glide towards me.

"Something else had my full attention. I didn't get a chance to eat much. But I did enjoy the dessert." Nathaniel words make me shiver. He stops to stand right in front of me. I can't take my eyes off him. If I wasn't so sore I would be all over him right now. He must have read my mind because he answered my silent thought by saying "Next time baby. Let's go get lunch."

"Yes." I'm too distracted by his presence to say anything else. It's weird the connection we have because as much as I love Quentin our connection wasn't as strong as me and Nathaniel's.

"Should we go now?" Nathaniel asks since I am still stuck in one spot practically drooling over him. I manage to rip my gaze from Nathaniel to Gia and see that she also couldn't take her eyes off Nathaniel. I clear my throat to get Gia attention. That didn't work.

"Gia I'm going to lunch. Hold my calls."

"Hmmm?" Gia say finally taking her eyes off Nathaniel and looking at me.

"I'm going to lunch. Hold my calls." I repeat.

"Okay. Yes. Hold your calls." Gia barely say as she return he gaze to look over Nathaniel again.

"Shall we?" Nathaniel holds his arm out for me and we leave my office. I can still feel Gia's gaze on us as we walk out the door.

I thought Nathaniel was taking me to my favorite restaurant the, Grand Lux Café, but we end up at Lawry's across the street from it.

"Expensive lunch."

"You're rich and still cheap."

"Rich but realistic."

"I'm rich and don't mind spending my money on my girlfriend."

"Girlfriend?" I ask raising my eyebrow.

"Would you rather I call you something else?"

"No I like girlfriend."

"Mr. Stock please follow me. Your booth is ready." The men say interrupting our intimate gaze.

We follow him to a booth that was secluded away from everyone else. They blocked one section of the restaurant off to give us the romantic setting Nathaniel must have planned.

"Flashing your money to seduce me Mr. Stock?"

"Depends. Is it turning you on Ms. Fairchild?"

"I was turned on when I opened my office door and saw you in that suit."

"Then it looks like flashing my money is working out for me."
"Indeed it is Mr. Stock."

"How is your day going so far?"

"It's going great. I'm looking into a new investment opportunity."

"Sounds good. Maybe I should hire you to do some investing for me."
"I can't possibly keep myself together that long around you to talk business."

"You're going to make me think you just want me for my body."
"That's one reason." I say giving Nathaniel a flirtatious smile.

"Keep flirting with me and I will bend you over this table and show all these people in here that you are mine."

My mouth drops wide open as my pussy get instantly wet. I can't even respond back because I'm to busy visualizing him doing exactly what he said. My mind is so far gone that I didn't even notice the waiter have come until he is walking away. I look up at Nathaniel and see his mouth moving but I hear nothing that comes out of it.

"What did you say?"

"Is it okay that I ordered for you?"

"Yes. Of course."

"I want to talk to you about something."

"Shoot"

"How do you feel about us starting back searching for information about who we are?"

"I don't know."

"You don't want to know?"

"I do. I'm just tired of running into dead ends."

"Maybe we will have a better chance looking together."

"Me and you or me, you, Arashi and Joel?"

"Me and you and Arashi and Joel. Maybe we have a better chance that way."

"Okay but I'm not going to put my life on hold to do it. I'm going to live as much of a normal life as I can."

Nathaniel nods in agreement as the waiter come back with our food. I block the rest of the world out when I see the big juicy steak the waiter sit in front of me. I lick my lips and look up at Nathaniel. He knew me so well. Well enough to know I love steak and I love a full meal. I never was one of them females to watch my figure. I don't even know if my figure can change. Either way I'm going to eat every bit of this steak.

Nathaniel smiles at me, he's happy to see how happy I am with his choice for me. He knew I liked to eat in silence so he just watches me dig in and shortly join me.

After we finish eating Nathaniel walks me back to my office. I feel like I just had my first date with a hot guy and couldn't wait to see what happened next. Nathaniel walks me all the way to my office door. I'm about to say thank you when Nathaniel kisses me. He kisses me slow and passionately. He wraps his arm around my waist and pulls me into him as he deepens the kiss. My legs begin to numb and I wrap my arms around his neck to avoid falling on my ass. When Nathaniel stops kissing me I'm too out of my mind in lust with him.

"I'll see you later baby."

"Yes." I answer knowing that it wasn't a question.

"I'll take care of dinner. Maybe we'll actually eat it this time."

"I promise not to distract you this time."

"I love your distractions. They turn me on."

I couldn't help the smile from ear to ear I give him. He rubs his fingers down my cheek and gives me a quick kiss before he leave.

"Later."

"Later." I say as I watch him walk out the door.

Chapter Three

The week went by fast. I am glad it is Friday and I finally can get away from Gia nagging questions about Nathaniel. She has been non-stop with questions ever since he took me to lunch. It's five o'clock and I am ready to run out of here. Friday's are always my busiest days with my clients because they make sure they get every question or request in before the weekend since I won't be in the office and I turn my phone off. It's not really a smart thing to do in my line of work but I refuse to not have time to myself. My clients understand and since I have not lost them money and my methods have been successful to them over the years, they don't demand my services over the weekend.

Arashi and I decided to get together this weekend since we haven't seen much of each other. I come to work, stay in my office and go home to Nathaniel every day. Arashi comes to work, stay in her office and go home to Joel every day. We barely get a hi or bye in by the end of the day. Things have really changed since Nathaniel and Joel came into our lives. We have to get back to being sisters.

"Adena I'm going. See you Monday." Gia says as she logs off for the day.

"See you Monday."

I lock up and head home. I hope Nathaniel doesn't have plans for tonight because I can use the extra sleep especially if we're spending the weekend with Arashi and Joel. Without the extra stress on my mind my guard must have been completely down because as I walk to the street to flag down a cab, I'm not prepared for the blow to the face that sends me crashing into the ground.

I shake off the blow and look up at the man that is evidently like me from the power behind his punch. He is about 6'2, 230 pounds, white, bold, and have tattoos traveling down from his neck all the way down to his hands. I know I need to question this guy but there's no way he's going to let me pin him down. I sit here and wait for him to make the first move. He looks unsure about if he has the right person or not, so I hold his gaze and begin to slide back away from him. He notice's my intentions and even though he is confused about who I am he decide to attack anyway. No more playing stupid. I flip back kicking him in the face. The blow barely moved him which told me he was either stronger than me or he is tapping into his abilities.

I don't have time to play and figure out what he wants. I know Nathaniel would worry soon if he hasn't started worrying yet. My cell phone started to ring as I thought that and I didn't have to look at it to know it is Nathaniel. To get this over with I have to tap into my anger more than I should have. Everything is suddenly red and I know my eyes have changed. I lung at him. He comes at me at the same time. When we are about to crash into each other, I flip over him, grab his head and yank his head off.

I don't have time to clean this mess up since it's still light outside and this is downtown Chicago. The strip is never empty. People begin to lurk around in surprise of what they just saw. Before the people have got a chance to really look at me, I grab my things and ran full speed to Nathaniel's place. To normal people I properly look like I vanished into thin air.

I make it to Nathaniel place and walk in on an outraged Nathaniel. He's pacing back and forth with the phone up to his ear until he noticed me standing in the doorway.

"What the hell happened?" Nathaniel snaps at me. He's not mad at me but I can see the worry all over his face. I pause before answering him. Nathaniel instantly blinks right in front of me. He arch my face to look at the bruise I imagine is there from the blow I took.

"I was attacked after I left work."

"In broad daylight? People had to be everywhere."

"Yes in broad daylight and yes people were outside."

"Did anyone see you or recognize you?"

"I don't know. I got out of there pretty fast but they probably saw me when I was on the ground from the blow he gave me when my guard was down."

"You can't go to work for a while. Whoever sent him will send more and they know where you work. You need to call Gia too and keep her out of the office for a while. It will be best if you both work from home for a little while."

"Yea. I'll call her in a minute."

"Where was Arashi?"

"She always leaves work early on Fridays. She doesn't think anyone should waist a whole Friday at work."

"We need to let Arashi and Joel know so that we can find the idiots who sent someone after you and make them beg for their useless lives."

"I like when you go into protective mood but we are going to see them tomorrow anyway. Can't we wait until then? I need to sleep and if you call them they will rush over here and sleeping will never happen."

"This is serious Adena."

"I know Nathaniel. Even if we did talk about it tonight, we don't know who he is, where he came from or where to even start. I'm tired Nathaniel, give me until tomorrow. Please."

Nathaniel stands there for a minute just staring at me. I know he is pissed and need to do something now but I need to sleep and process. My eye is killing me and I have blood on me. I just want to get in the shower and go to bed. Nathaniel doesn't move or say anything. I don't know what he's thinking about but I need a shower. I walk past Nathaniel but he grabs me and pulls me into a bear hug.

"Nathaniel I'm okay."

"I want to rip them apart. I'll die if something happen to you."

"I do have some fighting skills you know." I say trying to lighten the mood. All it does is make Nathaniel hold on to me tighter. "Hey. Nathaniel. I'm okay."

"I know. I felt like someone was ripping my heart out. It came out of nowhere. I was fine one minute and then a sharp pain hit me. I knew something was wrong. I knew it."

"Wait. You felt something wrong? I don't understand. How?"

"I don't know. All I know is that I needed to find you."

"We really need to find out what this connection is between us. It would be fucked up if you turned out to be my brother or something." I wasn't joking that time but it made him laugh.

"It wasn't that type of feeling Adena. I'm sure if were related Bruce would have said something."

"Bruce might not know."

"Bruce knows more than you give him credit for. You think Arobi would have trusted his secrets to a man who he didn't think can keep them at all cost."

Nathaniel was right. Bruce certainly knows more than the rest of us. There must be a reason why he hasn't told us what he knows or he is still trying to protect us from something.

"True."

"Come on. Let's get you cleaned up and in bed. We have a long day tomorrow."

"Does that mean you won't feel on my booty and tell me how soft my skin is?"

"As much as I want to. You're tired and if I feel on your booty I'm going to do a lot more to you."

"I think I can muster up some energy for you."

"Trust me. You won't be able to walk tomorrow if I touch you tonight."

"Tease."

Chapter Four

Nathaniel wasn't lying. Last night he fucked me in every position known to man. I think he even made a few up. Walking is impossible this morning. There is no way I'm making it out this bed without a wheelchair. Wiggling my toes is even a bad idea.

"I brought you some breakfast."

"Seeing that I can't walk because of your overly active sex drive."

"I warned you."

"Yes. You did. But damn Nathaniel I really can't walk. What am I suppose to do when Arashi and Joel come over here today."

"I'll carry you to the front room before they get here and I'll play hostess to whatever they need."

"Arashi and I can hear each other's thoughts. She's going to find out anyway."

"Then there is nothing to worry about then."

"Give me my food. I'm starving."

We eat breakfast and get ready for Arashi and Joel to come over. I can't do much so Nathaniel takes care of all my needs and carries me everywhere. I can get use to this.

Nathaniel sits me comfortably on the couch and gives me the remote so I can watch my shows. I barely settle on a channel when Arashi and Joel knock on the door. I take a deep breath because I know what's coming when Arashi see the bruise still present on my face.

"OMG it feels like forever since we all been together. I see much hasn't changed in Adena's choice of shows." Arashi is saying as she walks through the door.

"Don't hate on my shows Arashi. They're very entertaining."

"To you maybe. The rest of the……." Arashi stop talking in the middle of her sentence when she came around the couch and seen my face. "What the hell happened to your face?" Arashi snaps taking her eyes back and forth between me and Nathaniel.

"It's not that bad." I say trying to lighten the mood.

"Adena don't play with me. We don't bruise easily so either you ran into another one of us or Nathaniel got some explaining to do. Which one is it?"

"I ran into another one of us and Nathaniel has some explaining to do."

"What? When?"

"When I left work yesterday. He hit me while my guard was down and I decapitated him in return."

"Why didn't you or Nathaniel call me?"

"Nathaniel wanted too but I asked him not to since you and Joel was coming over today anyway and I was tired."

"Adena I don't give a shit about how tired you were last night. You should have told me."

"Arashi I'm fine. There was no need for you to rush over here last night when everything was fine."

Arashi was still railing but she sat down next to me and smacked my thigh. I wince from the pain not because her hit hurt but because I was still feeling the aftermath from last night.

"What the hell did he do to you? You're in pain everywhere. I can feel it like it's my own pain."

"That pain didn't come from my attacker." I said as I look up at Nathaniel with a huge smile on my face. I couldn't help but think back on everything Nathaniel did to me last night."

"OMG! Ill. I didn't need to see all that. Adena stop. Stop thinking about it right now."

"Sorry. Kind of hard to forget."

"I see that. Nathaniel really. That was a bit much wasn't it."

"Don't look at me. Adena asked for it." Nathaniel said.

"I'm sure she did. Can you walk Adena?" Arashi ask poking at my leg.

"AH! NO! Now stop poking me."

"That's what you should have told Nathaniel last night. I don't even think Quentin ever worked you that much doing sex."

"Arashi!"

"What? Sorry is Quentin still a sensitive subject?"

"He's not a subject. Why would you even say that?"

"I was just stating a fact. It's not my fault we have this weird connection to each other."

"Whatever."

"What did he look like?" Joel ask throwing me completely off with his question.

"Who?"

"The man that attacked you."

I went into detail telling them what happened and giving them a description of the men who attacked me. It was evident that it was someone neither Joel nor Nathaniel ever ran into in their line of work. Whoever he was, he was now another reminder that we are not the only ones out there and that we all weren't looking for the same thing.

"This happened right when you left the building?" Joel asked.

"Yes. I was just about to hail a cab."

"I can't believe he attacked at that time of day with everyone there to witness it."

"That's not the first time we've been attacked in broad daylight." I say remembering when we were attacked at Bruce's flower shop.

"That was inside Bruce's store. No one was there to witness it." Nathaniel counters.

"I'll be back." Joel announced and then jetted out the door.

"Where is he going?" I asked confused.

"Tracking." Arashi and Nathaniel say at the same time. They must have noticed the confusion still on my face because I still don't get what they are talking about.

"Joel has a six sense. He's good at tracking people. If anyone can tract where he might have come from its Joel." Nathaniel explains.

"That's why you wanted to call them yesterday?"

"Yes."

"You should have let him call us anyway." Arashi snaps again.

"Okay Arashi I get it."

Before Arashi could snap back at me Nathaniel phone rang. He picks it up but doesn't say anything. He just listens to the person on the other line. Arashi and I watch, waiting for him to say something but he never do. Before he hangs up the phone he looks up at me but I can't read the expression on his face. Before I ask what's wrong he was gone. Nathaniel left. I jump off the couch to try and follow but I'm stopped by Arashi.

"What are you doing? Let me go Arashi." I snap at her.

"He's probably just meeting up with Joel Adena."

"You don't know that. That phone call didn't look like it was from Joel."

"We won't know until he gets back. I'm sure you wouldn't be able to track Nathaniel anyway feeling the way you feel. You barely made it off the couch."

"Call Joel. Something is wrong. I know it. I can feel it."

"What do you mean?"

"Just call Joel."

Arashi reach for her phone to call Joel but before she can call him he was standing right in front of her.

"Calling me?" Joel asks Arashi as he rubs his fingers down her cheek. Arashi is too busy blushing to answer his question and ask my question about Nathaniel.

"Where's Nathaniel?" I ask getting angrier by the minute.

"He's not here?" Joel asks.

"No. I thought he was meeting you when got that phone call." Arashi say.

"I didn't call him." Joel says.

I start to pace back and forth. I know something is wrong. I could feel it. I feel it through my whole body. I know what Nathaniel meant when he told me yesterday that he knew something was wrong with me because he felt it like it was his own pain. I'm not in pain but I just feel wrong.

"Adena you ok?" Arashi ask.

"NO!" I snap. "Something's wrong. I can feel it."

"What do you mean you can feel it?" Joel asks me.

"I don't know. Nathaniel and I have some type of connection to each other. We don't know what it is yet. Yesterday when I was attacked Nathaniel felt my pain as if it was his own. He knew something was wrong and called me right when I was attacked. He told me last night but I didn't completely take it in until now. I can feel something is wrong. I don't feel any pain but I feel a lot of anger. I'm mad as hell and it's not just my attitude I feel."

"What happened when he got the call?" Joel asks.

"His phone ringed, he answered, and he didn't say anything he just listened to the person on the phone. Before the call ended he looked at me. I couldn't read the expression on his face but I felt something was wrong. He was gone before I could even ask what it was."

Joel looks confused and angry but there was nothing I could say to reassure him or tell him where Nathaniel is. I stay focus on the feelings I am feeling. Nathaniel is pissed. I try to pinpoint where he is but I get nothing. I try focusing more and feel a pull. Everything goes red. I can't hear or see Joel, nor Arashi. Before I know it I blink out to somewhere else. When I come back to, Arashi had a grip on my shoulder and Joel was holding on to her.

"What the hell was that Adena?" Arashi ask surprised. I don't think I ever did that with her before.

"I don't know. I was focusing on Nathaniel's anger and it brought me here."

"That must be some connection." Joel says.

"Where are we?" Arashi ask as she looks around.

"I don't……….." I start to say but am being pulled again by another wave of anger by Nathaniel. Everything turns red again and in a blink of an eye we were somewhere else.

"What the hell Adena. We barely caught you that time." Arashi scream.

"I can't control the pull. I can't pinpoint him either. Whatever he is doing, he is moving fast from place to place. He hasn't stop moving which is why we haven't caught up with him yet. Joel does anyone of these places look familiar to you?"

Joel takes a look around. We are still in Chicago but somewhere on the south side. We're standing in front of a yellow two story house. It looks like it has been recently remodeled. I watch as Joel look around the house to see if it is familiar to him.

"Wait a minute. I think we should hold hands. There's no telling when Adena will get another connection with Nathaniel." Arashi suggest.

Joel eyes get wide in surprise. Before he can tell us why I get another pull from Nathaniel. This time harder than the last. We blink out and are suddenly back at Nathaniel's place.

"I don't understand." Arashi say.

We drop each other's hand and try to figure out what was going on. I still feel Nathaniel but it feels different this time. He wants me. I can feel his need to hold me so I focus on it and blinks out. I end up in Nathaniel's bedroom. He's lying on the bed with his arm covering his face. I don't say anything I just go to him and lay on top of him. He instantly wraps his arms around me and squeezes me until I can't breathe.

"Feeling better?"

"Yes."

"What was that about?"

Before Nathaniel could answer. Arashi and Joel are busting through the door.

"What the fuck!" Arashi snaps. "What the hell was that Nathaniel? And Adena you worried the shit out of me just to end up in the bedroom. You couldn't have yelled back here to ease our fucking mind?"

"Arashi I figured you would sense me."

"Well I couldn't."

"What? Why?" I ask confused. We have always been able to sense each other and we sensed each other just fine a moment ago.

"I don't know Adena." Arashi snaps again.

"Why weren't you here when I got back?" Nathaniel asks me.

"Because you were dragging me across Chicago." I reply.

"Really?" Nathaniel says as he pondered that for a minute.

"What is this about Nathaniel? Who called you?" Joel asks.

"Someone I thought I'll never hear from again." Nathaniel answer.

"Meaning what Nathaniel?" Arashi ask with a frustrated tone.

"It was our foster father." Nathaniel says as he locks gazes with Joel.

"How did he even find you?" Arashi ask.

"He's been looking for us for a while. Evidently since we left. He eventually got in contact with Seth but they never finished whatever they started since Adena killed Seth." Nathaniel looks bothered. I want to ask what's wrong, but I can tell he don't really want to tell us this much.

"What does he want?" Joel finally asks.

"His wife died shortly after we left and he blames us. So I guess this is revenge for him. He managed to get in contact with some people like us through Seth before he died. The man who attacked Adena was one of them."

"So I guess it's time to pay him a visit." Joel says. I can see Joel wants to end whatever it is before someone comes after Arashi.

"That's what I was trying to do but I don't know where he is. The number he called me from was a burner phone and he destroyed it. He also managed to get away before I got to him. Which means he is probably with someone else like us. His next target is Arashi." Nathaniel said the one thing no one wanted to hear. He knows that will rattle Joel.

"More fun for me." Arashi says in her playful tone. I don't know why she is always so eager to fight.

"No. I'll deal with whoever he sends. We can't kill him anyway because we need to question him." Joel tells Arashi.

"You're not with me all the time you know." Arashi snaps at Joel.

"You don't have to worry about that anymore. You're working from home for now on and I don't want to hear your shit about this Arashi." Joel snaps back and storms out the room.

Arashi didn't say anything. She just stood there in shock for a minute and then went after Joel.

"What do you want to do now?" I ask Nathaniel.

"This is something Joel and I need to handle. I need you and Arashi to stay out the way and let us deal with it. You and Arashi also need to stay together so you both could stay here or at Arashi's place. It's your choice."

"Nathaniel you talking like you won't be here."

"I won't. He wants Joel and me. I won't let him come after you to get to us. We will track him and you and Arashi can protect each other if someone else comes. I rather both of you to be together."

"Nathaniel let us help. We're not two regular women you have to hide and protect. We can protect ourselves."

"I know Adena. Please don't argue with me on this. Just do it." Nathaniel pleads with me. I don't want to argue with him because I don't want him to go. I want him here with me so that I can know he is okay. I want him to hold me at night. I don't know how I will feel with him gone.

"You have to keep me updated. If you don't call me and tell me what's going on I'm going to track you down and kick your ass Nathaniel. I don't agree with this but I will do it for you only if you keep in contact with me."

"I promise to do my best."

"When are you leaving?"

"Tomorrow."

Chapter Five

I'm not ready for Nathaniel to go. He made love to me last night like it was our last night together. We never admitted love to each other but there is no other way to explain last night. We barely got two hours of sleep in.

We decided that I would go to Arashi house. We both know if I stayed here I wouldn't do anything but worry and think about Nathaniel. Especially being in his place with nothing but reminders of him.

"You ready to get this over with?"

"No. I want to stay in bed with you all day." It's the truth. I'm still hoping he won't leave.

"I know baby."

"What time did you tell Joel we will be there?"

"By noon."

"That's too early."

"The earlier we go, the faster we can get this over with."

"I know."

We get out of bed and start to get dress. We eat breakfast together and watch some of my favorite TV shows. It's going on 11 and I know it's time to go.

"Time to go baby."

I take a deep breath and wait a few seconds before I respond. "Okay."

We get up and head to the door. We're almost at the door when Nathaniel grabs me and give me a long passionate kiss. I know it was suppose to make me feel better but all it did was make me worry more.

"You're acting like we'll never see each other again Nathaniel."

"It's just hard for me to let go too. I don't want to go as much as you don't want me to go."

"Well then you better hurry back home to me then."

"How can I refuse that?"

"You can't. Let's get out of here so we can get this over with."

"After you."

We made it to Arashi house and I waited as Nathaniel got my bags out of the car. Since Arashi never locks her door we just walk in. When we walk in Joel and Arashi is standing in the foyer saying their goodbyes. I knew they were leaving soon. Just not as soon as we walked in the door.

I turn around to face Nathaniel. "Now?"

"Yes." Nathaniel responds.

"WOW ok." I say on another deep breath. I was really starting to feel like I was being ripped apart now.

"I feel it to baby." Nathaniel say responding to how I'm feeling.

"You sure this is the right thing to do because we shouldn't feel this way?"

"It's the only thing to do Adena. You promised me you wouldn't fight me on this."

"No. I agreed to let you handle this. Not that I wouldn't fight you on this."

"Adena please."

"You just said you feel it too Nathaniel. That means something is wrong."

"Trust me."

"I...I...do. But….."

"No buts Adena. Just trust me." Nathaniel pleads with me to just trust him. I want to but I just know something is wrong. I just look at him and nod in agreement.

"Thank you." Nathaniel says. He kisses me goodbye and leave out the door to wait on Joel outside.

"It's okay Adena. I'll make sure nothing happens to him." Joel said before he closed the door behind him and left.

I instantly drop to my knees and try to fight the pain I am feeling. I feel Arashi come to my side to make sure I am okay.

"Adena what's wrong?"

"Somethings wrong Arashi. I feel like I'm being ripped in half. I know they think they're doing the right thing but something is going to happen. Something is really wrong and Nathaniel knows it."

"What does that mean Adena? Joel is there with him. I'm sure he won't let anything happen to Nathaniel."

"And I'm sure Joel doesn't know what he's walking into."

"Don't make me worry Adena."

"I'm not trying to. I just want this pain to go away."

"Look at me Adena. Instead of channeling Nathaniel, channel me."

I try focusing on how Arashi is feeling. I close my eyes and block out thoughts of Nathaniel and replace them by focusing on Arashi. After a few minutes it works. I don't feel the rip from being away from Nathaniel anymore. But Arashi feelings of regret for letting Joel go wasn't better.

"Your feelings aren't any better Arashi."

"It's better than feeling like you're being ripped apart."

"Good point." I laugh.

"See you laughed. I'll say that's progress."

"Thank you Arashi."

"I do what I can. So now that we're stuck in the house. What can we do?" Arashi ask. I know it's not a question. She probably planned a year worth of stuff already.

"I can hear your thoughts Adena."

"Sorry. I got to get use to being around you again."

"Really? I miss you too."

Arashi and I kept ourselves busy so that we won't think too much about Nathaniel and Joel. Days passed and we still haven't heard anything. Then weeks. Now months. We both are at our breaking point. No more waiting for them to contact us. We decided that it is time to step in. We agreed to start looking for them tomorrow morning. We don't know where to begin to look so we decided that the earlier the better.

I decide to go to bed early tonight because I'm too anxious for morning to come. I hear Arashi pacing around the house because she can't sleep. She's been trying to call Joel every day and he has yet to answer her. I lay back and close my eyes. I'm on my way to sleep when I get a pull so strong I feel like every part of my body is being torn apart piece by piece. The pain is excruciating. I can't hold on anymore. I call out for Arashi.

"Arashi. ARASHI!"

"Adena. What's happening?"

"I can't hold on anymore. Hold on to me."

Arashi gripped my wrist and I locked my hands around hers. I give in to where the pain is coming from and in that second Arashi and I blink out to somewhere else. We land on our asses in what looks like a dungeon flooded with dirty water.

Arashi and I instantly got up ready to fight. We are back to back scoping out the room. That's when I feel it. Feel the pull again only it's not far away any more. It's still as strong as before.

I ran full speed towards the pull. I hear Arashi call after me but I knew she would follow. I don't know what to expect so I expect the worst and get ready for whatever awaits me. I make it to a small room covered in blood. I notice three men and leap in the air landing on one of the men. I wrap my thighs around his neck, flip him down and snap his head from his body with my thighs.

When I stand up I'm standing in front of a grey eyed Nathaniel who looks more pissed then happy to see me. I can't focus on his anger because man number two is behind me. Before he has a chance to do anything I extend my hand back, push my hand through his chest and rip his heart out without taking my eyes off Nathaniel. Arashi takes care of the third man and is already trying to free Joel.

"What are you doing here?" Nathaniel snaps. I don't answer him. I'm too angry. I just brake the chains that's' holding him and look at Arashi and Joel.

Arashi grabs Joel and come to hold on to me. I place my hand on Nathaniel and take us back to Arashi place. I'm still railing with anger. Everything's red. Arashi lets go of me and attend to Joel. I never remove my hand off Nathaniel. Without thinking I blink us to Nathaniel's place.

"You shouldn't have come for us." Nathaniel says but I still can't calm down yet to argue with him. His eyes are still a stone cold grey and mine are furious red.

All I want to do is kick Nathaniel ass and I know he can feel just how much because I can feel just how hard he's trying to hold himself back from doing the same to me. I'm ready. Ready to kick his ass until all of the sudden I drop to my knees and throw up.

"Adena. Adena are you ok?" I hear Nathaniel ask but I bolt to the bathroom and make it just in time to the toilet before I throw up again and again.

"Adena what's going on baby? Tell me what's wrong."

"Don't touch me. I'm fucking pissed at you. It's been months Nathaniel. Months."

"I know baby. I'm sorry. I'll tell you everything just let me take care of you."

"You're not coming near me like that. You're covered in blood. You need to get in the shower."

"Not until I know you're ok Adena."

"I'm fine." I snap as I stand up a little too fast and go crashing back down.

"Baby."

"I just need to lie down. I'm dizzy. I've been railing too long and to hard when you pulled me to you."

"Let's get you in bed and then we can talk about it tomorrow."

"Ok but seriously don't come near me like that. I'll never make it to the bed because I'll be running back to this toilet."

"Then hold your breath Adena because I'm not letting you walk."

"It's not just your smell Nathaniel. I can't stand to see you like this. The chains are still around your wrist." I point out. Nathaniel finally looks himself over and sees what I see. It still didn't send him running to the shower though.

He doesn't touch me but he watches me and make sure I get in the bed without collapsing. He blinks out of the room and seconds later I hear him in the shower. He moves at the speed of light because three minutes later he's in bed with me smelling and looking like a god.

He gently takes my clothes off. He leaves and came back with a bucket, water and soap. He washes every inch of my body until I am clean like a baby. He gently moves me from one side to the other of the bed as he changes the dirty wet sheets and replaces them with dry freshly washed ones. When Nathaniel is done he eases into bed with me and hold me tight until we fall to sleep.

Chapter Six

It's still night time. I can feel the rays of the moon shining down on me from the wide open window in Nathaniel's bedroom. I'm awaken by Nathaniel's hunger. His hunger for the juices currently flowing from my pussy. He ate me. Ate me like he's a starved man to his breaking point. He ate me like I'm his last meal and he couldn't have more.

My back is arched up towards the ceiling. My head is thrown back deep into my pillow. My eyes are rolled back into my head and my mouth is wide open. Nathaniel has my thighs pushed back and his hands gripping my thighs to open me wide for him. My feet are pushing into his shoulders trying to control the explosive feelings from each lick Nathaniel's tongue give my clitoris.

Nathaniel used his tongue to create specific designs within my walls. With each design Nathaniel marks his signature labeling me as his. In this moment I know that I am his. When I thought the feeling couldn't get any more mind blowing, Nathaniel tongue goes deeper into my walls. His tongue explores and finds new spots in new places the deeper he get.

I can feel my orgasm rising strong and hard. I'm ready to explode from the overwhelming sensation coming from between my legs. Nathaniel's tongue moves faster and harder within me. My back arches higher toward the ceiling. My head pushes back further into my pillow. My eyes feel as if they are never returning back to me.

I'm pushing my toes into Nathaniel's shoulder. My orgasm is rising faster and harder. I explode. My body slightly tenses together. My voice is stuck in my throat. My body falls limp to the bed. I give into the darkness that is taking me in.

"I love you." Is the last thing I hear before I blackout.

I'm awaken. This time from the sun rays shining through Nathaniel's window. I am still feeling the high from my explosive orgasm last night. I know Nathaniel is watching me. I can always feel his eyes on me. I don't open my eyes. I just smile and relax under the sun. Nathaniel kisses each of my eyes and I moan in appreciation.

"I made you breakfast." Nathaniel says. I slowly open my eyes to look at him. His eyes grow wide for a minute and then back to normal. I sit up so that he can sit the tray on my lap. He made me pancakes, sausage patties, and a cheese, turkey and tomato omelet. Just what I like and a tall glass of apple juice.

"Thank you."

"I never saw your eyes do that before. Do they do that often?"

"Do what?" I ask confused.

"Your eyes changed. They are a mixture of hazel brown and red. Different, but very beautiful." Nathaniel says in awe.

"What?" I move the tray off my lap so I can go to the mirror and see what Nathaniel is talking about.

I look in the mirror at my eyes. Nathaniel is right they did change. The red circled around my pupil and eased into the hazel brown of my natural color. It's not a bold red that would scare somebody. It's soft and beautiful like Nathaniel said. I move in closer to the mirror to take a deeper look into my eyes. The red was soft because it was mixed with another color. Grey. The same color of Nathaniel's eyes when they change.

"HOLY SHIT!" I yell. "Nathaniel." I call out. I don't know why because he was right there in the doorway of the bathroom.

"Yes."

"Look into my eyes. There is another color in them."

Nathaniel slowly glides over to me. I don't know how I can be still with him so close to me. He leans closer to me bringing his face right in front of mine. I try to stay still and look straight so that he can examine my eyes but the intense look of concentration on his face is making me giggle.

"Be still women." He says stealing me with his gaze.

"I'm trying. The look of concentration and interest on your face is making me laugh."

"I am intrigued. Grey." He finally says.

"What do you think this mean? I'm sure you didn't fuck your eye color into me."

"I don't know. Maybe it has something to do with this connection we have."

"Maybe."

"Go eat your breakfast. We'll figure it out later." He smacks my ass when I walk past him and goes back to the bedroom. I smile back at him and go eat my breakfast.

"We need to talk about what happen to you." I remind him.

"We will."

"When?"

"Soon."

"Soon when?"

Adena."

"Nathaniel you have to tell me what happened."

"I will."

"When?"

"Adena please."

"I won't let this go Nathaniel. What if some more people come?"

"They won't. I handled it."

"Really? How? Because I remember having to break you out of chains Nathaniel. Why were you even in chains? Why didn't you just break free? There were only three guys there."

"I killed some when I found him and you killed the rest when you came for me."

"So what happened?" I ask again.

"Adena just trust me. We'll talk about it later."

"I….I…do trust you. But……"

"No but's Adena. Just trust me."

I'm ready to fight him more about this but I don't. I look in his eyes. I know he's angry but I see something else. I see pain in his eyes. I know I have to wait for him to tell me when he is ready. I nod in agreement and finish my breakfast.

When I'm done eating I get out of bed and start my process of getting dressed. When I'm done getting dress I go to the living room to join Nathaniel. I walk over to the couch to sit next to him and he pulls me to straddle on his lap and hugs me. His hug is so tight I could barely breathe.

"Feeling better?" I ask.

"I am now."

I couldn't help the smile from ear to ear he put on my face with those words. I am happy. Happy to be here with Nathaniel after he's been gone for so long. We quickly got back into our routine. Nathaniel gives me the remote so that I can watch my favorite shows while he caress and watch me.

I hear them before they even knock on the door. Arashi and Joel are coming and Arashi is mad as hell. She bangs on the door non-stop until Nathaniel finally opens the door. She almost knocks Nathaniel down in her hast to get inside.

"What the fuck happened Nathaniel? And why can't Joel tell me anything?" Arashi snaps.

"None of your damn business Arashi." Nathaniel snaps back.

"My sister was attacked because of you so this does make it my damn business."

"The hell it does."

"Nathaniel I'm not leaving here until you tell me what the hell is going on. And if I leave, Adena is leaving to."

"NO! She's fucking mine. She's not leaving."

"Yes she is."

Nathaniel starts walking towards Arashi. He's stopped by Joel moving in front of her.

"Get the hell out." Nathaniel snaps at them.

"Nathaniel." Joel and I say together.

"Ok. Come on Adena." Arashi threatens.

"Keep fucking testing me Arashi." Nathaniel snaps at her.

"Stop talking to her like that." Joel tells Nathaniel.

I hurry over to put myself between Joel and Nathaniel. I put my hands on Nathaniel face and rub my fingers up and down his cheek to calm him down. He closes his eyes and pushes his face into my hand.

"You're not leaving me." He states to me.

"Of course not." I ensure him.

"Adena how can you stay with him when he won't even tell us what's going on?" Arashi is surprised that I would stay. She just doesn't understand what's going on. I've been putting pieces of this puzzle together while Nathaniel and Joel were gone. Nathaniel still hasn't told me anything but I figured out enough on my own.

"That's enough Arashi. It's none of our business."

"How can you say that?" Arashi ask.

I walk past Joel to stand in front of Arashi and place my hands on her folded arms. Because of my connection with Nathaniel, I am able to piece some information together and I feel like it's only far to share some of it with Arashi.

"I wasn't attacked because of Nathaniel. The day I was attached, Nathaniel was being followed by someone. Nathaniel had taken me out to eat that week and we were dressed professionally so it just looked like a business lunch of some sort. Whoever was following Nathaniel must have lost him at some point and decided to retrace his steps. He came back to the last place he saw Nathaniel which is at my office. He figured all he had to do was knock me out, take my office keys and look for information I had on Nathaniel. But when his blow didn't knock me out he realized I was like him. He either had to kill me or risk whatever they were planning to be compromised. Good thing I killed him first." I explained.

"Arashi it could have been anybody. It was just luck that I was the last person with Nathaniel. I'm just glad it was me and not my assistant."

"Why couldn't he just say that?" Arashi ask as she gives Nathaniel her death look.

"Do you want to stay and have lunch with us since you're here? Please?" I ask in an attempt to calm everybody down.

"I don't know. Do you still want me to leave Nathaniel?" Arashi ask Nathaniel.

"I'm sure if I say yes Adena would kick my ass." Nathaniel says before walking back to the couch.

"That's not an answer." Arashi yells after him.

"Let's just take it for what it is." I say and pull Arashi in the kitchen with me.

I set up the serving tray with fruit and cheese. I have Arashi pick out the wine and grab the glasses while I make some turkey and cheese finger sandwiches.

"Is there anything else I should know?" Arashi ask me while pouring the wine into the glasses.

"Maybe."

"What?"

I turn to face Arashi because I know she would look me directly in the eyes. We both have the need to give eye contact when talking to someone. It takes Arashi a minute to catch on, but I know exactly when she does because her eyes grow wide in surprise.

"HOLY SHIT! Grey. When did that happen?" She asks.

"This morning."

"How?"

"I don't know."

"Does Nathaniel?"

"No." Nathaniel answer as he and Joel join us in the kitchen.

"Joel look at Adena's eyes. They have grey in them." Arashi say in amazement.

Joel come around the breakfast bar and stands right in front of me. He looks into my eyes to see what Arashi is talking about. We all knew when he saw it. His eyes grew wide and he looks back and forth from me to Nathaniel.

"And you don't know anything?" Joel asks.

"We think it has something to do with the connection we have." Nathaniel answer.

"We definitely need to ask Bruce if he knows anything." Arashi says.

Nathaniel and I look at each other. We talked before about going back to the safe house to research and see what we can find out about our connection.

"Yea. We should go to the safe house." Nathaniel says.

"When were you thinking about going?" Joel asks us.

"I don't know. Maybe this weekend." Nathaniel answer.

"Yea. This weekend." I agree and smile up at Nathaniel.

"This weekend it is." Joel laughs and walks back into the living room.

We sit in the living room talking and laughing about old times. Arashi and I joke and tease each other about our past. Nathaniel and Joel joke with each other about their past. We tell stories and find a movie to watch. We laugh and joke about the movie together. It feels nice to be able to relax together and have a normal day. Whatever normal means for us.

Time has flown by. It's getting late so Arashi and Joel decide to go. Nathaniel and I offer for them to join us for dinner since we are ordering in. They decline and say they have some catching up to do. We knew what that meant. We hug and say our goodbyes. We agreed to meet up Friday and go to the safe house together.

Chapter Seven

The week had flown by. I'm going to the office today to get some things I need to take with me to the safe house. I don't know how long we will be gone but I want to stay on top of my work. I instructed Gia to continue to work from home. We would meet up twice a week over lunch to discuss what needs to be done for the clients. I gave her all my numbers and Nathaniel's so she can reach me in case of an emergency.

I leave the office to head back to Nathanial's place so I can finish packing my stuff. Since I have to pass a small grocery store, I decide to go in and get a few things to take with me to the safe house. I end up buying some more fruit and cheese. My junk food cravings have decreased since I have been staying with Nathaniel.

I'm on my way to the counter when I pass the pregnancy tests in the ale. I don't think it's even possible for us to get pregnant. If it was, surely Arashi and I would have been pregnant by now, considering the amount of sex we had in the past. We didn't use condoms or birth control because our bodies also reject everything that went in that didn't belong. We naturally healed ourselves.

Being pregnant would surely explain some of the things that have been going on with me. I stop the battle going on in my head and just throw the test in my basket. I went to the counter to check out. There aren't many people in here so there's no wait at the register. I'm in and out in no time.

I know Nathaniel have some things to do before we leave to go to the safe house so I don't know if he made it home yet. It don't take long for me to make it back to Nathaniel's place he's really not that far from my office. I place my bags on the breakfast bar and go to look for Nathaniel. I know he isn't here but I just want to check and make sure.

Ok I can breathe, Nathaniel's not home yet. So I grab the pregnancy test out my bag and head to the bathroom. I read the instructions on the back of the box and follow the directions. When I'm done I wait, and wait, and wait the required wait time before looking at the stick. "HOLY SHIT!" The test is positive. This has to be from something in my DNA right? I don't want to think too much about it or get excited about something that may not be possible. Nathaniel might freak out. Holy Shit! I have to get rid of this test before he gets back home.

I put the test back in the box and throw it in the kitchen garbage. I have to take the garbage out before Nathaniel get home. I should have time to finish packing my things first. It's too late. I hear Nathaniel when he comes in. I know he's watching me because I could always feel his eyes on me. He has a way of making a single stare that can make my body relax and yearn for him at the same time.

"Hey baby." He says.

"Hey." When I turn to look up at him, Nathaniel looks anxious or confused about something. If not confused, nervous. When he looks back at me I see him physically relax and take a deep breathe.

"I told Joel and Arashi to meet us here by three."

"Ok."

"Is everything ok?" He asks me. He comes behind me and wraps his arms around my waist.

"It is now." I respond with a smile. I turn around to kiss him but ends up running to the bathroom to hurl.

"Adena. Baby what's wrong?" Nathaniel asks, but I can't answer. I can't move my head from the toilet without feeling like hurling over and over again.

"Something's not right. We don't get sick. We have to hurry up to get you to the safe house." Nathaniel babbles on panicking.

I'm finally able to lift my head from the toilet and see Nathaniel pacing back and forth in worry. I'm about to say something but hurl in the toilet again.

"Adena. We have to go."

"I'm pregnant." I shout out. I go still at the same time Nathaniel freezes in spot.

"What?"

"I'm pregnant." I repeat. I don't know if I just need to get that off my chest but I finally stop throwing up. I notice Nathaniel is still frozen in the bathroom doorway so I got up to wash my face and brush my teeth. I turn to face Nathaniel and he's still frozen, staring at my stomach.

"I'm not sure Nathaniel. I don't know if we can even get pregnant and I don't want to scare you if it's not even possible."

Nathaniel drops to his knees but never take his eyes off my stomach. He doesn't say anything for what seems like forever.

"That would certainly explain the changes you been going through." He finally says. I walk over to him and drop to my knees to face him.

"Nathaniel I don't even know if it's possible for us to get pregnant. Something could just be wrong with me."

"Nothing is wrong with you. You're perfect." Nathaniel says with this huge smile on his face.

"Thank you. But I don't want us to get our hopes up Nathaniel. We need to know for sure. I took a pregnancy test today and it came back positive but something in my DNA could have made it say that." I babble on trying to convince myself that I'm not pregnant.

"Or you can be pregnant."

"I don't want anyone to know until we are sure."

"Then we'll make sure." Nathaniel simply state.

"Okay." I agree and put my head down. Although I'm excited I may be pregnant. I can't help but think that if it is possible I wish I would have got pregnant the tradition way. Like after I was married.

"What's wrong?" Nathaniel asks me. He cups my chin to raise my head so I can look at him.

"It's silly."

"Tell me."

"It's just that if I am pregnant I wish I would have done it the tradition way. You know. Meet a nice guy, get married and then have some kids."

"If that's what you want then it's not silly. Unless I'm not the nice guy you are talking about."

"Of course you are." I laugh.

Nathaniel pulls me over to him and sits me in his lap. He hugs me, kisses my forehead, and then rubs my belly.

"I love you baby." He says.

"I love you too. Unless you were talking to my stomach." I say joking around.

"Sorry. I love you too Adena." Nathaniel says with a grin from ear to ear. I gasp and smack Nathaniel in the stomach for teasing me.

We sit here enjoying the feel of each other. I never saw Nathaniel so happy. I can't help it. I smile back in excitement that we may have a little me or him growing in my belly. Time must have passed by because Arashi and Joel are knocking at the door. Nathaniel holds me a bit longer while rubbing my stomach, then hurries up to go open the door for them. I'm going back in the bedroom to finish packing our stuff. I grab our bags and head to the living room. Hopefully we can keep this a secret until we know for sure. It's going to be hard with Arashi reading my mind. I will have to block her out.

"What are you doing? Put those down. Now!" Nathaniel screams at me. We all look at him like he's going crazy. Nathaniel doesn't care. He walks over to me and takes the bags from me.

"Is something wrong?" Arashi asks.

"No." Nathaniel answer. "Men carry the bags. Women don't." Nathaniel says like this is his normal way of acting.

"Okay." Arashi say and rolls her eyes.

"Ready to go?" Joel steps in to ease the awkwardness in the room right now.

"Yes." I answer.

We leave Nathaniel's place and head to the safe house.

Chapter Eight

It doesn't take long for us to make it to the safe house. Arashi and I jump and leap through the forest like we use too giggling and playing in the trees. Nathaniel and Joel stay on the ground carrying all our things. Nathaniel refuse to let me, I mean us girls carry anything. They make it to the safe house before us because Arashi and I decide to swing and leap through the trees a little longer.

My playful mood doesn't last long. I know something is wrong because I can feel the pull of Nathaniel's anger. I instantly jump out the trees landing in a crouch and run full speed to Nathaniel's side. I freeze in spot when I see the cause of Nathaniel's anger. Quentin. Quentin is here at the safe house. It takes me a minute to figure out that I'm not seeing things.

"What are you doing here?" I ask.

"I came here to do some research." Quentin answer.

"Here in our safe house?" I ask. I'm still surprised that he would even think its ok. Why would he even want to come here?

"Arashi said you wouldn't be here for a while and said I can come here to do some research." Quentin responds. All eyes went to Arashi.

"What? That was a long time ago. I didn't think he'll still be here. Oh and thanks for throwing me under the bus Quentin." Arashi rolls her eyes and walk passes everyone to go in the safe house.

"I'm sure there's enough room for everybody. Besides we are all here for the same reasons." Bruce scoops in and save the day as usual.

"This should be weird." Dante says being his usual state the obvious self.

Nathaniel shook his head and goes up the stairs. I stand here a little bit longer before hugging Bruce and Dante. When I'm done, I go upstairs to check on Nathaniel. He's in my room laid across the bed. I go to him and lay directly on top of him. He wraps his arms around me and squeeze. I can't breathe but I'll hang in there a little longer.

"Are you ok?" I ask.

"I am now."

"Are you uncomfortable?"

"Adena I'm only uncomfortable if you are. I don't give a shit about him. I want you to be able to relax while we are here.

"I'm fine Nathaniel."

"I can feel how you wish he wasn't here Adena. Just like you can feel me, I can feel you."

"I feel that because I know you don't want him here."

"If you want to go we can go." Nathaniel says with a blank face. I know he's trying to hide the fact he wants to go.

"You want to go?" I ask.

"If that's what you want. I don't care. There's other ways to get information."

"But this is the best place to find the information we need." I state.

"Then we'll stay. The sooner we find the information the better."

We lay here holding each other a bit longer before taking a deep breath and going to join everyone else. Everyone's sitting around laughing and catching up. I notice that everyone tenses a little when we walk down the stairs. I go directly to the kitchen to find something to snack on. I get some fruit and cheese out the refrigerator. My need for junk has really decreased since I have been with Nathaniel.

"When did you start eating fruit and cheese?" Arashi ask coming up behind me.

"I don't know."

"Well if you're going to eat fruit we should at least have wine with it."

"Of course."

Arashi picks out the wine and I grab the wine glasses. I feel Nathaniel coming before he comes up behind me. He takes the wine glasses from me.

"I think water will be the better choice." Nathaniel gives me a warning look. I look ashamed because I know I shouldn't until I'm sure about what's going on with me and if I'm pregnant or not.

This is going to be a long weekend I thought to myself.

"Yes it is." Nathaniel responds to my thought.

"Yes it is what?" I ask him.

"You said this is going to be a long weekend and I agreed."

"I didn't say that Nathaniel. I thought it."

"You thought what?" Nathaniel asks me confused.

"I thought that this will be a long weekend. I didn't say it."

"Oh." Nathaniel says with no real emotion behind it. "*This isn't good.*" Nathaniel thought.

"*No it's not good.*"

"*You can hear me?*"

"*Yes.*"

"Are you hearing each other thoughts?" Arashi ask knocking us out of our back and forth thoughts.

"Yes." Nathaniel and I respond together.

"HOLY SHIT!" Arashi say.

"What?" Bruce asks.

"They can here each other's thoughts." Arashi just had to tell everybody.

Everyone just stares at us. Nathaniel and I were already frozen in spot looking at each other. We just walk away at the same time away from everyone. Nathaniel went out the doors leading to the practice area and I go upstairs to my room. I pace back and forth and then start to repeat over and over in my head 'this is crazy'. When I finally finish and take a deep breath I hear Nathaniel.

"This is crazy". I look around for him. He's not in the room with me. That's when I realize he thought it. I bolt down the stairs and go to where I know he is.

"You heard me all the way out here?" I ask.

"I guess so." Nathaniel answer.

"He heard your thoughts all the way out here from upstairs?" Arashi ask surprising me with her sudden presence. This is such not a good time for her intrusiveness.

"Yes." I say with a little more attitude than expected.

"How?" Arashi ask.

"I don't know." I reply. God we will never have time to figure this out alone here.

"What's going on?" Bruce asks. Great. Is the rest of the house going to come ask the same question too?

"Nathaniel heard Adena thoughts from upstairs, they have some type of freaky connection, and Adena eyes are changing colors." Arashi babble on telling all of our business.

"Do you mind if I take a look at your eyes Adena?" Bruce asks me. I want to scream yes. But whatever. We decided to come here and know we have to deal with everybody.

"Go for it." I say.

Bruce walks up close to me so that he can see what Arashi is talking about. He stares in my eyes for a few seconds then his eyes get wide. I know exactly what he sees. The grey in my eyes that came from Nathaniel. He looks back and forth between us and then focus back on my eyes.

"This is certainly new. I'll start researching now." Bruce says and goes back into the safe house.

Everyone else gathered around me to look into my eyes like I'm a science project or something. They all are surprised by what they see in my eyes. They look back and forth between Nathaniel and I. Nathaniel shakes his head in what seems like irritation and goes back in the house. One by one everyone goes back in. The last one standing outside is Quentin. He stares at me for a minute with a blank expression on his face and then follows everyone else back in.

I know it bothers him but I don't want to comfort him or try to explain it to him. I just want information. I finally decide to go back into the safe house and join Bruce in his research endeavor. I hope we find something soon so Nathaniel can know if we're going to have a baby or if something is really wrong with me.

Bruce stops around 11:30 and said he'll start looking again tomorrow. I bid him goodnight and continue my search for information. When I look up at the clock again it was 2 in the morning. I know I should stop and come back with fresh eyes in the morning but I just need to find something before I call it a night.

I'm beginning to doze off when I'm awaken by a familiar voice.

"You should get some sleep." Quentin says.

"You should be sleep."

"I couldn't sleep. Kind of weird sleeping next to your room."

"I don't know what to say. This is uncomfortable for everyone Quentin."

"I know and I know that's my fault."

"We all played a hand in it."

"Yea."

"I should go." I can already tell that talking with Quentin is a bad idea right now.

My responses are quick and I'm getting irritated with myself for being stuck here with both him and Nathaniel.

"Adena I'm sorry. I know it can't change what happened, but I am sorry."

"I know Quentin. I'm sorry too. I didn't exactly make the best decisions myself."

"But I should have. If I did things would be different right know."

"You don't know that Quentin."

"You're saying you would be with Nathaniel now if things didn't happen the way they did."

"I don't know Quentin. I won't say I wouldn't because it was bound to happen anyway. Nathaniel and I have a connection to each other. We didn't know what it was when we first meet but it's not doing anything but getting stronger and neither Nathaniel nor I want to fight it."

"So you think you're supposed to be with him?"

"No. I want to be with him. Not because of what happen between us but because I simply do."

"Okay." Quentin responds. He wants to say more. Whatever it is, he keeps it to himself.

"I'm not trying to hurt you Quentin. I just don't want to feel bad for feeling the way I feel for Nathaniel."

"I understand."

"Good." I turn around to leave before this conversation gets any more complicated.

"But Adena." Quentin begins to say. I turn around to face him and he's standing right in front of me. "One day. One day I will make you love me again."

"I do love you Quentin. I never said I didn't. But I'm in love with Nathaniel." I say and walk away.

"I go to join Nathaniel in bed. He's laid out across the bed in just his pajama pants. So I strip down to my underwear, climb in bed, wrap myself in Nathaniel's arms and go to sleep.

Chapter Nine

"What are you doing? They would hear." I say to Nathaniel trying to stop him from tearing my panties off. He's already ripped my bra off and is being more aggressive with me with each second that passes. "Nathaniel stops." I silently say. I'm trying to fight him off but it's only making him more aggressive with me.

Nathaniel looks up at me and I gasp from what I see. His eyes changed to that cloudy grey when he's mad but this time it was laced with red. I froze in my attempt to fight him off and struggle to tear my face away from his gaze. Before I know it Nathaniel rips my panties off. He still holds my gaze when he uses his thumb to begin a circular torture on my clitoris.

His touch instantly arouses me and a low moan escapes from my throat. I'm finally able to tear my gaze from him and focus on what his thumb is doing to me. My body is reacting to the need coming from my pussy. "Nathaniel please." I plead weakly as I try to push his thumb from my clitoris, but Nathaniel takes my plead as wanting more.

He move his head down so his mouth was hovering over me pussy. "No." I protest.

It's already too late. His tongue entered me fast and hard. Then slow and deep. I'm moaning louder as my body buck for more. My mind and body is being fucked separately and my arms soon fall limp from trying to push his head from between my legs. The only thing I have left is my voice. Yes my voice. "Stop Nathaniel. Stop." I say. My voice is just a whisper. There's no real demand behind it.

I'm about to give in. Just let Nathaniel finish so I can cum. I'll stop him after that. I close my eyes and put my head back finally giving in. Before my mind could adjust to my surrender, Nathaniel pounds into me sending me sliding up the bed. The pain registered in my head and I try to get away. Nathaniel grabs my ankle and pulls me back down to him. I start kicking at him trying to get away. He forces my legs apart and holds me down at the waist. He pounds into me again. Over and over. I can't move. The pain is too much.

"Nathaniel stop. Stop. Please." I yell. "You're hurting me. STOP!" I keep yelling hoping someone will come and get him off me. Nathaniel didn't ease up on me. His pounding starts to get faster and deeper. Tears are rolling out of my eyes. I'm yelling for him to stop but it was like he couldn't hear me. No one heard me. No one came in to help me. Not even Quentin who is sleeping in the next room from me.

I can feel my eyes changing. Everything is turning red. Then it gets cloudy from the grey that is present in my eyes. I'm about to attack Nathaniel. Fight him off me. I'm stopped by another force stronger than before. Nathaniel is pinning my arms down looking down at me. His eyes changing even more. The red becomes bolder and the grey was like a light protective shield over it.

When I thought the pain couldn't get worse, Nathaniel pounds in me again arching his hip. His dick managed to go deeper in me and I cry out. "NO!"

I manage to leap out of bed falling to the floor. I crawl over to the corner in panic trying to get away from Nathaniel. He's not behind me. It is suddenly light outside. I edge up to look and see what happened to Nathaniel. He's laid out in his pajama pants sound to sleep. I look down at myself and I still have on my bra and panties.

It was a dream. How? It felt so real. It still feels real. I'm shivering in fear. Tears are still running down my face. I still feel the pain from his pounding in me. It couldn't have been a dream.

I hear Nathaniel turn over in his attempt to reach over for me. I freeze not wanting him to find me. He raises his head and looks around the room for me and was in shock when his eyes finally found me.

"Adena what's going on? Why are you balled up in a corner?" Nathaniel asks. He's completely clue less to what he just did to me. I'm not going crazy. It happened. He hurt me.

I don't answer him. I just stay frozen in spot in hopes that he wouldn't come near me. When I don't talk or move Nathaniel gets up and come towards me. I panic and push myself further into the wall.

"What the hell Adena? Talk to me." Nathaniel says. He walks over to me. I bolt. I run full speed out the room. I can't stop. I run out the safe house. I'm running full speed through the forest in my underwear. I'm almost to the street when Nathaniel catches me and wraps me in his arms.

"NO!" I scream. "Let me go. Let me go." I yell at Nathaniel trying to fight him off me.

"Adena. Baby stop." His words triggered what happened in my head. I replayed it over and over in my head. I hear Nathaniel gasp and immediately let me go. I fall to the ground pushing myself back a few feet away from Nathaniel.

Nathaniel doesn't try to stop me. He stands in that same spot frozen. He looks horrified by something he saw. I'm still shivering from replaying what happened over in my head. Nathaniel had no clue what had happened. I had no clue if it actually happened. It was clear that it was a dream but the feeling felt so real.

I hear the others coming. I don't want them to see us like this. I push my fear of Nathaniel back and go to him. He immediately steps back.

"I hurt you."

"It was a dream. It's…its okay." I stutter.

"You're fucking shivering Adena. It's not okay." Nathaniel snaps.

"I'm okay." I go over to Nathaniel to try and prove it. I'm still afraid of him. But I'm more anxious to go before the others make it to us. Nathaniel looks down at me. His face is tense in anger and his eyes glared with pain. I know he needs to see I am really okay but I have to get us out of here first. I hear Arashi call my name and Panic wanting to be somewhere safe from everyone. Suddenly I blink us out and we are back at Nathaniel's place.

I let Nathaniel go and go to the bedroom closet to put on some jeans and a t-shirt. I take a deep breath before going back to Nathaniel. He's still standing in the same spot staring at me. I fiddle with my fingers and go to him.

"I hurt you."

"Yes. But it was a dream Nathaniel."

"Are you sure?" Nathaniel says lifting my wrist to expose bruises I have yet to notice. I look down in surprise and remember when Nathaniel held my arms down and pounded into me. I yank my wrist from his hold and step back. Nathaniel takes a step towards me and holds my gaze. I am still staring at him when I feel pain coming from between my legs. I wince and look down. Nathaniel is poking me with a single index finger softly. Each spot he pokes cause a moment of pain. I step back again.

"That doesn't feel like a dream." I can hear the anger radiating in his voice.

"Nathaniel don't"

"Don't what?"

"Get angry."

"Am I scaring you?"

"Yes."

"Good."

"We don't know what's going on with us Nathaniel. It was a dream. I was dreaming." I snap at Nathaniel.

"If you were dreaming, then what was I doing?" Nathaniel asks while slowly walking up on me. I don't like the look in his eyes so I walk backwards away from him.

"What are you talking about?" I ask.

"It just so happened you was dreaming what I was doing to you in my dream. You were dreaming exactly what was going on in my head." Nathaniel is yelling at me.

"Nathaniel stop." I yell back. "You didn't mean to hurt me."

"Yes I did."

"What? You don't mean that Nathaniel."

"Yes I do Adena. It was my dream. It was what I wanted. I have been holding in so much anger since…" He pauses. "I wanted you. I wanted you to take me how I was. Take me without me having to hold back. I wanted to release some of my anger inside of you." He finished.

"Nathaniel tell me what happened. What happened when you went after your foster dad?"

"No. I don't want to talk about it."

"You need to talk about it Nathaniel. Tell me."

"No."

"Nathaniel fucking tell me. We can't get past this if you don't." I snap.

"You're saying you'll leave if I don't?"

"I'm saying if I'm pregnant you could have hurt our child. You need to tell me what's going on with you or yes I will leave. I can't take any more dreams like that if I'm pregnant."

"Adena." Nathaniel reaches out for me.

"No Nathaniel. Tell me." I say and move out of his grasp.

"I told you I will. Just not now."

"Why? Holding it in is clearly not helping you."

"I don't want to think about it right now. I just want you and our baby. I want to celebrate us not think about him."

"But how can we celebrate the baby if I'm too scared of you to be near you?"

"I'm sorry baby. I didn't mean to hurt you. It was just suppose to be a dream."

"I know that Nathaniel. But were connected now and without knowing anything about the changes we are going through, don't you think it's best to put everything out on the table?"

"I just want to find out more about us and the baby before dealing with shit from my past. My past can wait. My future can't." Nathaniel says and places his hand on my belly.

I put my hands on top of his and look into his eyes. "Your past is hurting your future. Keep it to yourself and you will jeopardize your future."

Nathaniel put his forehead to mine and take a deep breath. We stand still for a few more minutes just taking in the presence of each other. Nathaniel finally pulls away and go sit on the couch. I watch him sit down and then went to join him.

"He's my real father." Nathaniel finally says.

"Who?"

"The man who adopted me and Joel."

"How?" I ask a little confused and shocked.

"He was with my mother before he was with my adopted mom. My mom was supposedly the love of his life when they were together. She died giving birth to me and my brother. My dad blamed us which is why we ended up in the system. He eventually decided that he wanted to keep the memory of my mom so he decided to find us. When he found Joel and I, he adopted us. He didn't know that Joel wasn't my brother." Nathaniel paused looking up at me. "Adopting us didn't make him feel better. He hated us even more especially since Joel looked nothing like him or my mom. He wanted to torture us because he blames us for the death of my mom and for the death of his wife after we ran away."

"Does he know now that Joel isn't your brother?"

"No."

"Does Joel know?"

"No."

"Why?"

"That stuff happened to Joel because he didn't look like me, my mom, or that fucking bastard of a dad. And now he was tortured because I didn't tell him the truth about us."

"He deserves to know Nathaniel."

"I know."

"Than what's wrong?"

"I figured out we are born in twos. If I have a brother out there, then so do Joel. I've been keeping him from finding his real brother." Nathaniel explains.

"I'm sure he'll understand Nathaniel. Besides you only found out shortly after we all met."

"Exactly. I could have told him and he could have made his own decisions on choosing to help a girl I liked save her boyfriend or going his separate ways to try and find his brother."

"I understand where you coming from but I don't think he would hold it against you Nathaniel."

"I don't know."

"I still don't understand why you let them torture you like that."

"It was the only way to get information out of him about my mom. When he was torturing us he was talking about her."

"Oh."

"I know I shouldn't have let them because Joel didn't deserve that. The bad part about it is that I don't want Joel to know. He may not be my real brother but he's still my brother to me."

"And if he stops talking to you, you lose two brothers."

"Yes."

"Nathaniel don't keep this from him. Tell him and give him time to deal with it. I'm sure he'll come back to you when he's ready."

"Yea."

"Yea." I say and kiss Nathaniel. "I love you."

"I love you too."

As much as Nathaniel wants to touch me he doesn't. He knows I'm still in pain so he just caresses my belly. I don't want him to touch me down there but I do want to feel his affection. He must have read my mind because he starts to caress my face.

"It's not nice to listen to other people thoughts." I laugh.

"I don't want to hurt you again."

"Unless you're about to start having visions about strangling me I think we're safe." I joke with him.

"Not funny Adena. I don't want to be angry with you and something happen to you."

"Trust me. After what happened I don't want you to be mad at me either."

"Good."

"You know. In that dream of yours your eyes changed."

"Grey. Yea I know."

"And red."

"What? They were red too?"

"It was scary as hell. I wonder do I look like that when my eyes change."

"Why would my eyes change?"

"Why wouldn't they? Mine did."

"Because you're pregnant. It could be the baby making those changes in you."

"And we are linked somehow. So it's possible for you to change to."

"We need to get back to the safe house so we can do some real research."

"You need to talk to Joel."

"I will."

"Before. Call him here so that you'll can talk privately Nathaniel. Don't let another day go by without telling him the truth. He deserves to know." I pleaded.

"Okay."

"Really?"

"Yea really."

Chapter Ten

Nathaniel calls Joel and ask him to come over so that they can talk. Joel and Arashi are already on edge trying to figure out what happened this morning. So I call Arashi and ask her out to lunch so I could explain what happened.

I also decided to meet up with Gia for a quick follow up on business. I know Nathaniel needs some time alone to think about how he wants to tell Joel everything. I hug and kiss him on my way out and tell him not to worry too much.

My meeting with Gia is short as expected. We wrap things up and I head back out to meet Arashi at Grand Lux. Although she has a track record of being late, I know she would be on time today because of Joel. Of course I'm right. Arashi is already waiting for me when I arrive.

"Is there a reason you and Nathaniel couldn't tell us this story at the same time?" Arashi ask. Ms. Drama can't stand not knowing what's going on.

"Two different stories." I reply as we head up to our usual booth.

The waiter takes our orders. I order a bottle of Sangria with our food. I figure we both will need it after I tell her what happened with me and Nathaniel.

"So tell me what Happened." Arashi jumps right in. She never misses a beat. I don't know how we made it all these years being connected.

I go into detail telling her about what happened. I told her how it turned out to be a dream but since we are connected it was somewhat real too. I watched her face as her facial expressions often changed from surprise, horror, and anger. There is no specific order either. I tell her we're more desperate now to find out information about our connection even more. I left out the part about us thinking I'm pregnant. That will have to wait until another time.

"Wow." Arashi looks in horror. I wait for her to take all the information in and pick a specific emotion. "I don't know if I want to kick his ass or stay the hell away from him." Arashi finally say.

"I know the feeling."

"I wonder what Nathaniel is talking to Joel about." Arashi hints to me. I knew she wanted to know. It must be eating her up not to know.

"He's telling him about what happened to them and the truth about them not being brothers."

"Really?" Her eyes light up in wonder.

"Yea."

"What happened with the whole adopted parent's thing?"

"I'll let Joel tell you that. That's not my story to tell."

"Adena."

"I can't Arashi. I'm sorry."

"Fine." Arashi pouts.

When our food come we eat, drink, and talk about when we first met Joel and Nathaniel. Arashi reminded me how I was playing hard to get with Nathaniel and I reminded her how easy she was with Joel. We're laughing and having a good time when I feel Nathaniel's need for me. It's so strong I have to hold on to the table to stop from blinking out in front of all these people.

"Adena. What's wrong?"

'It's Nathaniel. Something's wrong. He's pulling me. Pulling me hard."

"You're going to blink out aren't you?"

"Yes."

"We have to get away from these people."

"I don't know if I can let go of this table."

"I got you. You ready?"

I take a deep breath and nod. Arashi grabs me and practically rips me from the table. She pulls us out of sight as fast as she can without making people suspicious. When we make it out of sight, I give in to the pull. Arashi and I blink into Nathaniel's place. Nathaniel is standing frozen in spot in the living room and Joel is radiating with anger from across the room. I go to Nathaniel's side and hold his hand.

"Adena you knew about this?" Joel snaps at me. He walks toward me. Nathaniel instantly moves me behind him and get angry.

"Leave her out of this Joel." Nathaniel snaps.

"What's going on?" Arashi ask. No one answers her. Joel keeps his eyes on us and we kept our eyes on him. "Joel. What's going on?" Arashi ask again. Joel storms past her and leave. Arashi looks back and forth between me and Nathaniel and then finally locks her gaze with me. She holds my gaze a bit longer then goes after Joel.

"Arashi." I call out to her but she was already gone. "Nathaniel what happened?"

"He didn't take it so well."

"I can see that Nathaniel."

Nathaniel turns and face me. I can still feel the anger radiating from him. He's pissed. If I didn't know any better I'll say he's pissed at me. Nathaniel drops my hand and walk away. I decide to just let him cool off. Besides it will give me a chance to check on Arashi. I stand still and focus. Focus on Arashi. Although we haven't used our connection as much as we use to I'm sure it's still there. She's my sister.

I concentrate on her. I have to focus hard on the need to see her. The need to make sure she is okay. It takes a few minutes but I finally blink out. I don't know where I'm at. I don't even recognize this place at all. It's someone's apartment. It's a small place with all the basics. I don't dwell long on this place. I go search for Arashi in this apartment. I find her in the bedroom with Joel. She's consoling him. Both their heads snap up when they realize I'm there.

"What the hell are you doing here?" Joel snaps at me.

"I wanted to make sure you were okay." I respond calmly. It wasn't a complete lie. I am checking on Arashi but I also care that Joel is okay.

"You knew." Joel snaps.

"Yes. I'm sorry Joel. It wasn't my place to tell you. We had just met and Nathaniel asked me to keep it to myself." I explain.

"He should have told me."

"I agree. He just didn't want to lose you Joel. He didn't want you to think he would treat you different because you were no longer brothers and he didn't want you to be mad at him."

"It's a lot to take in. I'm pissed he didn't tell me. I'm not that little boy he keeps seeing me as."

"He knows that. He feels like everything that happened to you has been his fault. He thinks that if you weren't accidently placed as his brother you would have been better off." I tell him.

"What?"

"He blames himself. He was expecting this reaction from you. He prepared himself for you not talking to him again."

"I will never stop being his brother. But I can't deal with his feelings right now. We both have things to figure out and I think it's best we go our separate ways for a while."

"Please don't Joel." I plead. "We can find out information together. We're all looking for the same thing."

"But we're not getting anywhere because we're too worried about each other. Nathaniel can research what he needs to at the safe house. I will do what I'm good at and start tracking down information on my own."

"Are you going to at least talk to Nathaniel before you go?" I ask.

"No. You can tell him."

"I think he would rather hear it from you."

"I know the feeling." Joel reply. Joel gets up to leave. He walks past me then stops to look back at Arashi. He reaches his hand out to her. I look over to Arashi. I didn't expect him to take Arashi with him. I'm ready for this. Arashi gets up and walk toward us. She stops in front of me and holds my gaze. This is the one time I hated I can't read her thoughts. She hugs me and joins Joel.

Chapter Eleven

Weeks have passed since Joel and Arashi left. Nathaniel and I went back to the safe house to find some type of information about us. We are more determined now than ever to find it. Nathaniel and I are taking turns going back and forth from the city to the safe house to get things we need to get by. We haven't spent much time together. When one of us rested the other was researching. There were times when I feel asleep in the library from researching all night. Everyone is walking on egg shells around us. They just leave us alone and let us have the time we so clearly need.

The only thing we know so far about ourselves is that we are born in twos. If this is true, Nathaniel and Joel are not the only one missing a brother. Quentin and Dante are both missing brothers or sisters. We haven't told any of them yet because we don't want to get everyone worked up and it might not be true.

Today was like any other day. We get up, eat breakfast, and head straight for the library. We decide to take different sides of the library. There has been nothing weird in the history books we looked in that would give a clue when we first got here. We don't know whether we were born here or brought here. We even thought that our mothers may have been some kind of government experiment. That's not so farfetched to me.

We have been searching for hour's non-stop. Nathaniel finally stops and go get some rest. He kisses me and leaves the library. I last only a couple more hours and fall out on the book I'm reading. I don't think I sleep for long when Quentin wakes me up.

"I can start looking if you want to get some rest." Quentin says.

"I'm okay. Thanks."

"Well at least let me assist you."

"Okay."

"You two have been hitting it hard since you got back. Is there anything particular you're looking for?"

"We want to find information about our connection. It started off with just a pull now it's getting stronger. Our connection is stronger than what Arashi's and I have ever been."

"It can be because you two are the older sibling or because you belong together."

"What?" I say in shock. I can't believe Quentin thinks Nathaniel and I belong together.

"You not the only one who does research in here Adena."

"No. I know that. How do you know the older siblings are the strongest?" That's the first time I heard that one.

"Based off my experience with others, the oldest tends to be the strongest. If there is no sibling then your strength is your own. Not divided."

"But Arashi and I don't know which one of us is the oldest."

"That's obvious Adena. You are."

"And the reason you're so strong is because you don't have a sibling?"

"Yes."

"Okay so how do you explain Nathaniel? He's just as strong as you are."

"Because of your connection."

"I don't understand."

"If you two haven't noticed yet, you can tap in and out of each other's strength. I don't know why you're connected to each other but it's obvious by the change of your eyes that something is going on with you two."

"So you think Nathaniel and I belong together."

"Hell no. I think something about your relationship with him is changing you both. Something is changing within you. It's not just a connection anymore. It's something more."

"Like what?"

"I don't know. I'm assuming that's what you're looking for unless there is something you're not telling anyone." Quentin asks. I stop breathing for a minute because yes there is something I'm not saying. I'm pregnant.

"No. There's nothing." I say instead.

"Well let's find out."

We start researching some more. I am glad that Quentin is here helping me. Nathaniel and I haven't really been affectionate with each other since we got back to the safe house. He's dealing with his feelings about Joel and I'm dealing with mine about Arashi. We don't necessary blame each other. It's just our past and future is colliding and we're not sure how to handle it.

It didn't take much for me to fall back into my feelings for Quentin because they never really left. Since we been in the library researching we caught up on lost times. Quentin made us dinner, and when I got cold he used his hands to rub up and down my arms to warm me up. It felt good to be touched this way. I missed it but from Nathaniel. I couldn't get Nathaniel out my head for some reason so I stepped away from Quentin and started researching again. Eventually I fall asleep. I know when I went to sleep I was at the table. But I'm woken by the sound of Nathaniel's voice.

"Adena what the fuck are you doing?" Nathaniel snaps. The anger that's radiating from him is causing a painful pull in my stomach. My eyes shot open in confusion. I'm laid on the library couch wrapped in Quentin arms. "Get the hell up Adena." Nathaniel snaps again.

"Nathaniel it's not what you think." I say jumping to my feet.

"Really? You're not fucking lying in the arms of your ex?"

"I fell to sleep at the table reading Nathaniel not in Quentin arms." I can feel Nathaniel's anger growing. It feels like someone is ripping open my stomach with their bare hands.

Nathaniel's focus went from me to Quentin. I know what he wants to do so I made a step towards him to stop him but his anger increases, making me drop to my knees.

"Nathaniel please stop. You have to calm down." I plead but it only seems to get worse. "STOP!" I shout.

Quentin jumps up off the couch and immediately come to my aid. I try pushing him away but the pain was too unbearable. All I can do is hold my stomach and ball up on the floor.

"Adena what's wrong?" Quentin asks in a panic.

"Get the hell away from her." Nathaniel snaps at him.

"Nathaniel please." I plead again. "You have to calm down." I whisper.

"You idiot. You're hurting her." Quentin says standing to confront Nathaniel.

"Quentin don't. I can't take any more anger. Please walk away." I ask Quentin.

"I'm not leaving you like this and I'm not leaving you with him when he can't even see he's hurting you." Quentin snaps at me.

I was about to tell Quentin to just go when Nathaniel grabs him and throw him across the room. I grab Nathaniel's leg and try to stop him but he kept walking and dragging me with him.

There is only one way I feel I can get to him now that I may regret later. "Nathaniel stop. You're hurting the baby." I call out to him.

Nathaniel stops in his tracks and look down at me. My eyes are filled with tears and I am still holding my stomach with my other arm. I feel it when Nathaniel's anger decrease and he replaces it with regret and sorrow.

I want to tell him its okay but I can't. The pain in my stomach isn't as strong but it is still tearing at my stomach. I need to get away from the mixed emotions going on with Nathaniel. I need some air.

I manage to get up off the floor. I don't want to address what happened. I don't want to deal with Nathaniel right now and I certainly didn't want to deal with the shocked look on Quentin face from what he just heard me say. I just want to get away.

I walk past Nathaniel without looking his way and leave the safe house. I get as far away as I can. I go deep into the forest to sit at the top of one of the trees. I overlook Illinois and take in the smells around me.

This connection between Nathaniel and I is becoming more inconvenient by the day. I'm not sure raising a child like this is a good idea. I stay up here in the trees for a couple of hours trying to calm my thoughts down. I decide to just give it a rest for tonight and see how I feel in the morning. So I go back in the house and go straight to bed.

Chapter Twelve

I am woken up by Nathaniel famous breakfast in bed routine. It's not going to change the attitude I have this morning but I get up and eat it anyway.

"I'm sorry." Nathaniel says. He watches me closely for my reaction.

"I know." Is all I can say.

"I know you're mad at me. I can feel it."

"Really? Does it feel like something is being ripped from your stomach?" I ask in a calm tone that is laced with the anger still steady inside me.

"Baby. I'm sorry. I wasn't trying to hurt you."

"But you did. Even after I begged you to stop. I dropped to the floor because of the pain you were causing but you could only focus on Quentin who by the way was trying to help me."

"You were in his arms Adena. Lying down comfortably with him."

"I told you I didn't lay on the couch with him. I fell asleep at the table reading. Quentin must have moved me to the couch and laid me down with him."

"Which is why I wanted to kill him."

"I understand that. You need to understand that your anger physically hurts me. You need to control your temper until we can figure out how to break this damn connection. I won't keep taking silent beatings from this connection."

"Baby. I'm sorry." Nathaniel set next to me on the bed. He massaged my shoulders and ran his fingers down my spine. I missed his touch so much.

"Why haven't you touched me since we been here?" I finally ask.

"I don't want you to feel uncomfortable."

"Why will I be uncomfortable with my possible baby father touching me?"

"Because your ex would hear us."

"And you're worried that I won't enjoy myself because Quentin is here?"

"No. I just don't want you to be thinking about him while I'm inside you."

"I won't."

"You're sure?"

"Why would I be?" I ask and immediately wish I didn't.

Nathaniel starts to replay the dream over in his head. Especially the part when I told him to stop because they would hear. He zoomed in on the face I made when I was trying to stop him. I was looking towards Quentin's room.

It was true at that time. I didn't want Quentin to hear us but I remember giving in to Nathaniel need to pound me to death. I decide to give him a taste of his own medicine and start to replay how I gave in to him. I replayed the moans of want and need I made over and over. I feel Nathaniel stiffen behind me.

"I only think about you when you're in me Nathaniel." I say. I push the tray to the side so I can turn and look at him.

"Adena." Nathaniel whisper.

"Hum?"

I am overwhelmed with need and I want Nathaniel to meet every one of them. I sit here patiently waiting to see what he will do. His eyes look me over slowly. Watching my chest move up and down in desperation. He watches as I clinch my legs tightly together to control the feelings coming from my pussy. My hands grip the sheets to stop myself from touching myself.

I watch Nathaniel rise to his knees and look down at me. My mouth cracks open to relieve some of the air trapped in me from my heavy breathing. Nathaniel uses his thumbs to slowly move across my nipples. I moan and throw my head back pushing my chest out for more.

Nathaniel just sits there watching me. Teasing me with his eyes. I lift my hands to my chest and squeezed my breast with as much pressure that I can take.

"No." Nathaniel stops me. "Spread your thighs."

I follow his orders and spread my thighs. I moan from the feel of my panties moving against my pussy.

"Yes like that. Now reach back and grab your ankles."

I close my eyes and do as he says. The feeling is intoxicating. The longer I wait for Nathaniel to touch me the wetter I get. I can feel the moisture on my panties. Feel the juices pushing out of me as I wait.

I feel the slight touch of Nathaniel's fingers at my hip bone. He gives a small tug and my panties fall apart. The moans coming from me get louder. The wait is driving me crazy.

"No matter what, don't let go of your ankles." Nathaniel instructed.

I open my eyes to look up at him. I try to figure out what he's going to do but Nathaniel has figured out a way to block me from his thoughts.

"Don't move Adena."

"Ok."

Nathaniel edge slowly down to lay on the bed. I watch as he positions himself between my legs. His face is right beneath my pussy and he is extending my need to be touched when he blows air onto my folds. I struggle to keep still. I don't know how much longer I can keep this position before I let go and sit on his face.

"Nathaniel."

"Shhhh baby."

My body starts to tremble. Nathaniel uses his fingertips to lightly scratch up and down my thighs. I moan and lean my head back. Before I know it Nathaniel pushes my thighs further apart. I fall onto his mouth and he immediately began to lick, bite, and plunge into me.

I try keeping my hands on my ankles but the assault his tongue is giving my pussy is making me shake uncontrollably. When Nathaniel plunges his tongue into my pussy he has to grip my thighs to keep me from moving. I ride his mouth like a crazed virgin who can't get enough.

"OH MY GOD NATHANIEL!" I scream. I can't comprehend the technique of his tongue. It's pushing into areas I didn't know existed. It's poking me in places that make the room spin. His tongue is an erotic toy I just can't get enough of.

I explode, screaming out the intensity of my orgasm. I manage to keep my hands on my ankles before falling limp on Nathaniel's face. My body is still jerking from my orgasm when Nathaniel decides to give my clitoris a few more licks.

"Ah...please…mum….natha……" I stutter. I am too sensitive to take anymore. I still can't move and Nathaniel has yet to tell me to let go of my ankles.

I'm about to say something when Nathaniel suddenly flips us over making me let go of my ankles and start his licking game all over.

"OH NO! I can't Nathaniel. Please. Nathaniel." I scream out. Before I know it, I explode again.

I lay out on the bed. I feel like I have just been drugged. I feel Nathaniel as he pull me to the edge of the bed and spread my legs.

"It's not over yet baby. Stay with me." I hear Nathaniel say. I nod in agreement before my eyes start to drift back into the darkness.

My eyes shot back open when Nathaniel slams into me. My body lifts towards him and then falls back limp to the bed. Nathaniel moves fast and hard until he finally explodes inside me. I keep my eyes open long enough to see Nathaniel collapse next to me. I'm out as soon as his body touches the bed.

Chapter 13

When I wake up, the moonlight was shining bright in my room. Staring at it while laying here full of love and satisfaction put's a smile on my face. I don't know why, but I feel enlighten. I look over to Nathaniel and suddenly I can't think about what my life would be like without him. Even as he sleeps I feel his strength, his love and his protection over me. I can't remember the last time I felt this full with someone. The feeling is overwhelming and steady at the same time. I do not know who we are in general, but in this moment I don't care as long as I get to keep this feeling forever.

I wish I could lay here and sleep beside Nathaniel until morning, but I'm feeling too energized to fall back to sleep. Instead I think I'll do some more research. I head down to the library just to take a look at the scrolls again. I know we went through them already but it doesn't hurt to look again. Sensei Arobi always talked around the message he gave. Maybe he did the same with the scrolls. Maybe we all looked past something.

Blinded by my good mood, I can't help the giggly way I enter the library. I go straight to the scrolls without noticing Quentin silently watching me from the corner wall.

"You're in a good mood despite what happened a few hours ago." Quentin says with a hint of disappointment in his voice. I get why. I'm just not in the mood to entertain it right now. He might not agree with what's going on with Nathaniel and I but it's between us.

"Yes I am. Look Quentin I know you don't agree with what's going on. But it's really between Nathaniel and I." I keep my eyes on the scrolls as I pull them off the shelves. I'm not ready to have this conversation with Quentin. I haven't even talked to Arashi about it yet.

"And I'm just suppose to be the punching bag when trying to defend you when Nathaniel is mad?" I can feel the anger radiating through his words. He has been on the other side of Nathaniel's anger and mostly due to the choices I made.

"No Quentin. You're not. I'm not saying Nathaniel temper is justifiable. We all are just handling what's going on the best way we can." I take the scrolls and walk over to the table to review them again. I know Quentin needs more from me. I just don't think it's a good idea to have this talk while he's worked up like this.

"You're pregnant?" Quentin asks me
with what sounded like disgust in his voice. I
can feel a little of my good mood I was
holding on to fade away. The anger that
replaces it comes out full force in my
response.

"Yes. Quentin. I. Am."

"And let me guess. You're happy
about it?" Before I can react to the words he
just said to me, he put his hand up to silence
me. Silence me like he owns me or something.
As I flatten my palms on the table I can see
the room changing colors to match my anger.
I know he can see my eyes changing but he
keep talking. "Have you considered that all
our mothers died giving birth to us? Then
where does that leave your child? In the same
position we are in."

As angry as I am, his questions quickly
register and I unconsciously sit down and start
to think about the future of my child. What
will happen with him or her if I die and we
never figure out who or what we are? The
thought saddens me and I feel the tears run
down my face.

I look up at Quentin and watch his
face expression change as his anger turns into
regret. I don't have a response to his
questions. I never considered dying to give life
to my child. I put my hands on my stomach in
a way to protect my child. Protect it for what's

to come. How can I stop this from happening when I don't know why it's happening?

"Adena I…"

"It's okay. I needed to hear that." I get up to leave to go lay back down with Nathaniel. I want to feel that same love and protection I felt not too long ago. The reality of our situation just became more real than I could have even imagined. I don't know how Nathaniel is going to react to this news.

"Adena don't go. I shouldn't have said anything. I let my anger get to me." I appreciate his sincerity but his words were truthful.

"It's ok Quentin. I'm not mad. I just need to go lay down for a while." I reach down to grab the scrolls so that I can put them back on the shelf since I don't know when I will have the energy to really search through them again. I didn't see Quentin move but he's standing in front of me reaching for the scrolls. I take a deep breath and just hand them to him. When I let go to leave, one of the scrolls sticks to my hand. I try to shake it off but it won't get off so I just try pushing it off my hand.

The scroll rips apart and I almost scream my surprise. I can't believe I just ripped Sensei Arobi scroll. Oh my God, oh my God, oh my God is all I can chant in my head as I drop to the floor with the scroll. "Oh no! What did I do?" I whisper.

"Don't worry Adena. We can put it back together." Quentin's trying to settle me down, but I can't calm down. It's just another problem I created.

I start crying and breathing hard. What is wrong with me? Why are all my choices turning out to be bad ones? Now I possibly can't save my own life.

"Adena calm down. It's okay. It's just a piece of paper." Quentin says as he holds up the scroll for me to see. That's when I saw it. The scroll didn't rip apart. It looks like two scrolls put together. I wipe my tears away and carefully take the scroll from Quentin. I get up and go back to the table with the scroll.

"What is it Adena?" Quentin asks.

"I don't know yet. Look." As Quentin get up to make his way to the table I start to slowly pull the scroll apart. It's another scroll in Sensei Arobi writing. He did hide secret scrolls. He hid them within the other scrolls. We both watch in silent anticipation as I slowly pull it apart. I was careful not to mess it up. When it finally came apart, Quentin and I look at each other for a long minute. Both of us hesitant to read it. We finally looked down at the scroll and I pray it have the information we need. Surprising, Sensei Arobi wrote the scroll in English. Unlike all the other scrolls that are in Japanese.

Scroll 4 of 13
****

"My only regret is that I'm not around to guide the girls while they become the women they are meant to be. If these scrolls are found and I have not yet told the girls who they are then I moved on from this life. I'm hoping that Adena and Arashi do not encounter any problems down their journey for these scrolls and I hope they find the information or guidance they need within these scrolls. I myself know how hard it is to obtain the information I have. If not for the relationship with their mother, I still will be in the dark about a lot of things. I have learned a great deal of things from Merloni and a lot more from raising the girls myself. My previous scrolls contain information about the girls as they grew up. Adena and Arashi both had many abilities beginning at birth. I just wish Merloni would have been able to guide and teach them as she often talked about. I'm doing my best raising the girls with human ways as Merloni wished. But I fear the girls would have to come to terms with who they are to protect themselves in case something happens to me."
****

I flip the scroll back and forth looking for more information. Nothing. Nothing was there. "Is that it? It can't be it." I begin to babble.

"There's probably more scrolls hidden. We just have to find them."

"You're right." I get up and gather every scroll we have. I look up at Quentin wondering why he just standing there. "A little help here." I insist.

"Sorry. I'll take half." Quentin begins trying to find duplicate scrolls as did I. So far nothing.

"This can't be it. He said himself there are more. Come on. Come on." I start yelling out my frustration. I must have been loud because Nathaniel is here and I can feel his anger zooming in on Quentin. He's on his way towards Quentin when Bruce and Dante enter the library.

"What's going on?" Bruce asks.

"I was just about to ask Quentin." Nathaniel says.

"Nothing. I found this Bruce but I can't. I can't find the rest of them." I Interrupt Nathaniel. My hands are shaking while trying to show Bruce the hidden scroll we found. "There has to be more right?" Bruce looks at me before taking the scroll. He grabs my hand to stop the shaking.

"Let's see Adena." Bruce finally says.

"Adena, what the hell! You're shaking." Nathaniel says.

"Arobi did leave something. There has to be more. We looked but that was it. We have to find the rest Nathaniel. We have to." I kept babbling.

"Okay okay okay baby. We will. You need to calm down. Come here." Nathaniel pulls me into him and hugs me tight. I instantly squeezed him for support. There are so many things going on in my head and we just found our first clue to who we are. I know if we can find the rest I can find out the outcome of my life and possibly my baby as well. I'm no help like this so I attempt to calm down. To take deep breaths and control my emotions. "You okay baby?" Nathaniel asks me as I breathe in and out of his chest following his rhythm.

"Yes I am now." I look up into Nathaniel eyes to reassure him. Then I turn toward Bruce to see his reaction to the scroll we found.

"Where did you find this Adena?" Bruce asks me without taking his eyes from the scroll. I knew when he was done because like me, he turned the scroll back and forth looking for more. When he realizes that was it, he finally looks up at me.

"It was attached to one of the other scrolls like it was glued together or something." I explain.

"Well it does say scroll four of thirteen." Dante adds.

"I see. Now that we all are a little calmer let's try the other scrolls again for duplicate's." Bruce suggests.

So we all grab scrolls and split up in different sections of the library. Nathaniel stays with me to keep me calm. Instead of getting myself worked up again I watch Nathaniel try different ways to see if the scrolls have duplicates. Watching his facial expressions change like a kid deep in thought when trying to figure something out made me smile.

Nathaniel looks over at me from the corner of his eyes with the same determined look and smile at me. I try to hold in the giggle that's fighting to slip out of me.

"Okay I'm getting nothing." Nathaniel finally says.

"Me either." Dante says next.

"Adena what happened earlier? How did you find out about that duplicate scroll?" Bruce asks.

I look over to Quentin and reach for Nathaniel hands. I just know he's about to get upset.

"Well, Quentin and I were having an argument and he said somethings to piss me off to the point my eyes were changing. Then he asked some questions that made me think and I settled down a little. I start crying when

I was about to leave. The page was stuck to my hand. I tried shaking it off but it split. I thought I ripped it but it turned out to be a duplicate page." I explain.

"You made her cry!" Nathaniel snaps at Quentin.

"It's ok Nathaniel. He was just making a point. One I should have thought about myself." I stop Nathaniel from going towards Quentin and try to keep him close to me to avoid him overreacting.

"What point?" Nathaniel snaps again.

I swear he just like getting into it with Quentin. I wish he will just let this go or now. "Well talk about it later. Let's concentrate on these scrolls for now. Please Nathaniel." We all waited for Nathaniel to calm down. It took a minute but he finally let it go.

"Were your hands touching the scroll when you got angry?" Dante ask.

"I think so. I wasn't really paying attention." I respond. "Why?"

"The heat from your hand may have separated the page from the scroll. When you get angry and your eyes start to change, your body warms up as well. The warmth or steam depending on how angry you were could have separated the pages." Dante explain.

"Yes. It could have." Bruce agrees.

"Let's try some old fashion steam first since you haven't mastered control of your anger yet." Bruce suggests.

"Okay. I'll go boil some water." I happily go to the kitchen to get away from the death stare Nathaniel is giving Quentin right now. We're never going to get anywhere if these two keep fighting.

Chapter 14

As I'm waiting for the water to boil I look out the window at the sunrise. It's one of the most beautiful sunrises I ever seen. It's one of the reasons Arashi and I built this safe house here. I miss Arashi and hope her and Joel come back soon.

"I'm sure they're okay. They will come back when they're ready." Nathaniel says as he wraps his arms around me.

"I know. I just wish I can talk to Arashi about what's going on with us. I especially want to tell her about our news."

"Why don't you reach out to her? Use the connection you have and bring her to you." Nathaniel suggests.

"I would love that but I think she would be mad if I just yank her here not knowing what they are doing." I laugh.

"Focus and see if you can get a mental connection with her and ask."

"We're too far apart. That won't work."

"Well pull her here Adena. I'm sure she'll get over it when you tell her the news."

"I think so to. Ok I'll do it now." I feel excited to finally be able to tell Arashi.

"Ok. I'll take the water to the others."
I watch him as he take the water from the
stove and goes back to the library.

I'm excited to finally be able to tell
Arashi what has really been going on with me
and Nathaniel. It's been hard keeping stuff
from her. I walk back and forth going over in
my head what to say. Asking myself will she
be mad or will she be happy for me. I was just
about to convince myself not to do it when
Nathaniel interrupts my thoughts.

"Just do it Adena. You're driving me
crazy." Nathaniel complains.

"Get out of my head." I try to sound
demanding, but of course it doesn't work on
Nathaniel.

"Make me. Call Arashi." Nathaniel
taunts.

"I am. Be quiet."

I focus on Arashi. Blocking out
everything and everyone else. Once my mind
I clear I'm was able to pin point my focus on
Arashi. I have to ground myself not to pull
myself to her but pull her to me. We have
never tried this before but I guess now is a
better time than ever to try. I got her. Come
on. Come on. It feels like Arashi is pulling
away from me but I finally get a strong hold
on her and yank her to me.

I'm about to rejoice in my ability to
pull her to me until I open my eyes and see

Arashi bent over on the floor beat up and hurt.

"Arashi. What happened?"

"Adena we have to go back. Now. We have to get Joel." Arashi panics. She grips on to me. Pleading with me to go back. Joel must be in real trouble. I look up and see Nathaniel walking back into the kitchen for me.

"Please Adena. Now. Joel is in trouble." Arashi snaps.

I look up at Nathaniel knowing he will be furious for what I'm about to do. I blink out with Arashi taking us back to the place I pulled her from. I hear Nathaniel scream no and felt the anger resonating from him as he try to catch me before I left.

"Arashi where are we? What's going on?" I ask confused. We were in someone's basement. A very nice basement at that. I don't understand what exactly is going on.

"Be ready. They're coming." Arashi says.

"Who's coming?" I ask but Arashi didn't have a chance to answer. Before I knew it we were surrounded. "What the hell did you two get into?" I snap.

"Not now Adena." Arashi instantly went full force towards the men surrounding us.

"I don't have time for this." I close my eyes and focus my anger on the men surrounding me. When I open my eyes the room is red with grey smoke blurring everyone vision. I lift my hands towards the sky lighting the grey smoke with fire. The men didn't know what to do. They hesitate to strike so I look at them and smile. Finally they gain the courage to fight me. I wait until they are close to me and bring my hands down covering them with the firing smoke. They turn into ash instantly. I turn around and start a slow walk towards the men attacking Arashi. I just touch them one by one as I walk past them turning them all into ash. I finally make it in front of Arashi and I can see the fear in her eyes. Not of the men I just killed but of me. I calm myself down and slowly clear the air of the smoke and fire I created. Last I get rid of the fire red eyes I know is present right now.

"Adena?" Arashi says my name like a question. I know she's wondering if it was me or if I lost control of myself again.

"I'm good Arashi. What is this?"

"Joel and I were following another lead while looking for his brother. Someone tipped Joel off about this place saying his brother might be here so we came to try it out. Instead we were ambushed. Ambushed by a lot of people like us. We were captured and they were about to take us somewhere when you pulled me out. Joel is still in trouble." Arashi says in a rush.

"Arashi why didn't you try to call for me so we could help you both? You shouldn't have checked this place out alone."

"We didn't think there was a problem Adena. You think we would have intentially walked into a place full of others like us? We were looking for his brother not to lose our lives."

"I get that Arashi but neither one of you have bothered to contact us at all. If I wouldn't have pulled you to me. We would have never known you were captured."

"I know. Right now we need to get Joel out of here safely. Please." Arashi pleads.

"I doubt that's all of them Arashi. By the look of this basement this is a big place to search without getting noticed. The only way to find out exactly where Joel is we would have to get captured ourselves."

"Well let's just get to Joel and fight our way out. That shouldn't be hard to do especially with what you just did to them." Arashi say in a rush to save Joel.

"That would be a good idea if us getting beat in the process wasn't an option." I snap.

"When did you start caring about taking a beating Adena? Why are you fighting me on this? If it was Nathaniel you would be gone already."

"You're right but things have changed Arashi. I just can't jump into fights anymore."

"So Joel life doesn't matter to you?
It's not important enough for you anymore?"

"His life does matter to me Arashi and
we will get him back but his life is not the
only one at stake right now."

"I'm fine. You know I will heal soon
Adena."

"Not you either Arashi."

"Then what the hell are you talking
about Adena? We don't have time for this."

"I'm pregnant." I blurt out. It silenced
Arashi. She stands there in shock of my news.
Her eyes went down to my stomach and then
they slowly rose up to me. She just stares at
me for a minute and then starts to cry.
"Arashi what's wrong?"

"Nothing. I just don't know what to
do Adena. I just found out I'm going to be an
Auntie at the worst possible time right now.
I'm happy for you but also I...I...need to save
Joel."

"I know honey. Okay let's go save
Joel." I finally agree.

"No Adena. What if you get hurt?"

"I'll be fine. Let's just revise our plan a
little. Instead of getting ourselves caught let's
kick some ass and force them to tell us where
Joel is. Let's work off a little steam like we use
to." I smile and hold out my hand for Arashi.

"Okay. Let's go." Arashi agrees on a
deep breath and take my hand.

We walk up the stairs with the intent to kill. No sneaking through the house. No worrying about what's going to happen to us. We just have one goal. Kill everyone that gets in our way. Arashi is fueled by the need to save Joel and protect her unborn niece. I'm fueled by the need to protect my family. As far as I'm concern they all should be very afraid.

We walk side by side down the halls with no real destination in mind. My eyes glowing red and Arashi's glowing blue. We have never controlled our abilities with this much control before. We are feeding off each other's need to protect this family. Nothing is getting in our way.

We make it up the stairs and through the long hall of the house. We should be worried about no one attempting to kill us but we are too focused on what we need to do. We make it to a staircase at the end of the hall. A weird place to put a staircase but who am I to judge.

Without hesitation we head up the stairs. The quietness is starting to get to me. Where are they and why haven't they attacked us yet? I look behind me just to make sure no one is behind us. I got a feeling that we're not going to like what's waiting for us at the top of the stairs. When I look ahead at Arashi I still see the same determination we had when we left the basement. Instead of worrying I snap back into the mindset of our plan. The faster we get this over with the sooner we can get back to our lives. Besides, I might only have nine months left to live anyway.

In the middle of me babbling to myself in my head the air shifted a little. Someone is coming full force at me but it's too late to react. I put my arms out to protect my stomach from the blow coming my way and close my eyes. I wait a couple more seconds but the hit never comes. I open my eyes and see the man frozen in spot. I look over to Arashi and she is standing stone cold with her finger pointing at the man in front of me. Her eyes still iced blue.

I look back at the man in front of me frozen in spot just in front of my stomach. Without hesitation I spin kick him in the chest breaking him in over 100 pieces. It's just what I need to get my focus back. Arashi powers are growing and this is the first time I seen her this focused on a mission.

We continue our stride up the stairs. The closer to the top we get the more of their presence I feel. All of them like us with abilities. None of them seem worried about the power emanating from Arashi and I. That doesn't stop us. We continued on our mission to save Joel without a blink of an eye. We finally make it to the top. The room is filled with others like us. I can feel their presence but it wasn't as strong as the amount of people in this room. That was until the ones who were holding back made their presence known when we entered the room. The strength of their abilities hit us so hard we both got knocked back a few feet. Although Arashi determination and focus did not break, the reality of this situation hit me fast and hard.

I look around at the man and woman starting to surround us. Most had smirks on their faces watching us with looks of anticipation. I can feel their want to hurt us. The excitement they get from our timely arrival. They were waiting on us.

"Arashi we need to go."

"Not without Joel." Arashi attacks.

"Arashi NO!" I scream and try to go after her but it was too late. Arashi try to throw her ice at one of them but he absorbed it somehow. After he absorbs it, he looks up at Arashi and smile. Similar to the taunting smile Arashi give's people when she's fighting. That's when the reality of our situation sinked in with Arashi.

We move closer together. Positioning ourselves back to back. There is no way we're getting out of here on our own. I guess we will find Joel after all. We're about to end up exactly where he is.

"Arashi no matter what stay with me. We have a better advantage that way."

"Adena I'm sorry for getting you into this with me." Arashi gives me her if we don't make it apology.

"Arashi I'll kick your ass for this later. Let's kick some of their asses now."

"Let's." I can hear the smile in her voice when she says it. We might be in over our head but we're not going down easily.

We crouch down in position to attack. They all start to slowly walk towards us. No one in a rush to attack us and no one scared enough to worry about us either. We are about to attack full force when Nathaniel and Quentin appear in front of us. I can feel the density of their combined powers in the air. It's enough to make the others in the room take a step back. The look of disapproval in Nathaniel eyes when he looks down at me told me I was in trouble when we got out of here.

Nathaniel focuses his attention back to the others. They look scared. I can feel the worry they have about Nathaniel and Quentin being here but it didn't stop them. They all attack at once but are quickly short stopped by Nathaniel hand. He froze them all in spot. They tried moving but their bodies are in Nathaniel control. They all went flying with the flick of Quentin hand. I never felt so much power before. Quentin and Nathaniel together are like an unstoppable force.

"Where's Joel?" Nathaniel asks.

"Where is my brother?" Nathaniel goes for them all. He walks up to them one by one freezing them in spot and slowly ripping them apart for the others to witness and hear their screams.

Quentin also attacks. He takes them out with one blow. His strength crushes and smash whoever gets in his way.

Arashi and I stand in this one spot and watch in fear and amazement ourselves. We look at each other and then back at them.

"I would stop killing my men if I were you." A voice says from behind us.

We all turn and look at the man crazy enough to make that threat. To our surprise it's Joel. He looks different. He looks better. No scars on his face. He is very well dressed and groomed it appears. I would say he's been treated very well by his captures.

"Joel what's going on?" Arashi ask.

"Joel?" The man says as if he were asking. "Oh you must be referring to the men I have with my face. He's also shocked to see me as well."

"Where is my brother?" Nathaniel demands.

"I would say I think he's more my brother then yours." The men say and focus his attention on Nathaniel. "I didn't expect my little brother to bring so much trouble into my home."

"Where is he?" Arashi snaps.

"He's safe. Joel is not a prisoner here. He can leave whenever he wants." He responds.

"Then why is he still here?" I ask.

"I'm here." A voice says. We wait to see who it was. When he finally comes out from a back room it was Joel. Arashi ran to him in a hurry to get him away from his look alike. "It's okay Arashi. I'm okay." Joel says as he wraps Arashi in his arms.

"Joel what's going on? Who is he?" I ask.

"This is my brother. My twin brother Luke." Joel answer.

"Then why would your twin brother attack us?" Arashi snaps at Luke.

"I was simply protecting my home. You're the one who's trespassing. Not me." Luke responds with a slight smile on his face.

"We came here peacefully and your men attacked us." Arashi snaps back.

"What did you expect them to do when a men that looks like me walks in the front door and they know it's not me? My men are trained to attack first then ask questions. We are not all as friendly as you may think." Luke says.

"Well since he's free to go Joel lets go." Nathaniel says.

"Nathaniel I'm staying." Joel states. "I came here to find my brother and I did. We're not done talking. He knows a lot about who we are and can help us figure some things out. He can help me find out who or where I came from.

"What do you mean you have been talking? How much could you have talked about while I was fighting to get to you?" Arashi ask.

"When they took me to Luke you can only imagine the surprise on our faces to see each other. We look just alike. Luke already knew he had a brother out there. He didn't know he had a twin. Yes we are born in two's but we all don't come out looking alike. So this is a first in the eyes of both of us." Joel tries to explain.

"In that time of revelations did you think to come back for me instead of leaving me to die." Arashi snaps.

"I didn't leave you to die Arashi. Luke said you will be ok."

"Well they would have brought you to me before killing you." Luke smiles at Arashi.

"Look at me Joel. Did you leave me there with them because you trust him?" Arashi anger is coming out full force. Her eyes changes back into ice blue and she is breathing hard.

"Arashi calm down." Joel tries to calm her.

I go to Arashi and place myself between her and Joel. "Arashi it's okay. Calm down. Just breathe." Arashi eyes slowly start to change back. She kept her eyes on Joel and then focused on me.

"I thought. I thought…." Arashi started to babble.

"I know. I understand. Let's just get out of here. We can talk about it later." I guide Arashi back to where Nathaniel and Quentin are standing.

"Arashi" Joel calls out.

"I guess we'll be seeing each other again someday." Luke interrupts.

That was enough for Arashi to go off. She ran full speed blinking in and out towards Luke. She blinks in front of him placing her ice cold hands on his chest. She was slowly freezing him from the inside when somehow Joel pulled Luke into him and hit Arashi with a blow that sent her flying across the room. Before she went through the wall Quentin caught her. She could barely breathe and had two sets of fist bruises seared into her chest.

"Joel what the hell are you doing?" Nathaniel snaps.

We watch as Joel and Luke separate from each other. They were able to merge into one person. Something no one has ever seen before. Not even the men surrounding us. They are as confused and surprised as we are.

"Well that's a first." Luke says.

"Arashi. Arashi I'm sorry." Joel says. He's on his way towards Arashi when I placed myself in front of him. "Adena move."

"No Joel. You hit my sister." I snap.

"Adena move." Joel screams. Joel hands go up to move me himself and I get ready for a fight. Before Joel hit can come my way and my hit go his way Nathaniel spin me out the way and put himself in Joel face.

"Nathaniel. I'm just trying to talk to Arashi. I don't want to fight." Joel says.

"I don't want to talk to you." Arashi can barely talk from the blow she took from them.

"Looks like you pick the wrong side." Nathaniel says. He's angry Joel would attack Arashi like that. Someone he loves.

"I'm not choosing sides. I'm just trying to find out who I am." Joel responds.

"Well you do that." Nathaniel says.

"Who's picking sides now?" Joel asks Nathaniel.

"I'm on the same side I always been on." Nathaniel responds.

They both just stare at each other. Joel content on finding out more about himself and Nathaniel trying to accept Joel decision.

"Can we just get out of here?" Arashi finally ask.

"Yea sure." I say and go to Arashi side. Arashi, I and Quentin wait for Nathaniel and Joel to end their staring battle but it never came. I walk up to Nathaniel and put my hand inside his.

"Nathaniel lets go." I whisper to him. Nathaniel never takes his eyes off Joel. He just nods in agreement. I focus on the safe house and we all blink out.

Chapter 15

Nathaniel hasn't been himself since we got back to the safe house. I know he wishes Joel would have just come back with us but he also knows that Joel needs to find answers for himself.

The last couple of days went by in a breeze. The mood everyone is in is still the same. We all are walking around each other trying not to talk about the elephant in the room. Where is Joel? Why hasn't he reached out to us or just reached out to Arashi? Although she's acting like she is ok, I know she's hurt. She wants to be happy about Joel finding his brother but not at the expense of losing him. To be honest we have no idea how to comfort her so we just go with the flow of whatever mood Arashi is in.

"Adena you up for some training today?" Arashi ask me in the process of me thinking about how to let her know everything will be ok.

"Yea. Sure." I say without thinking.

"No you're not Adena." Nathaniel snaps at me. I was about to protest until I saw the look in his eyes and the burning stare he gave towards my stomach. I wasn't even thinking about our baby. I could have hurt it.

"He's right Arashi I shouldn't."

"Nathaniel I'm not going to hit her in the stomach. I wouldn't do anything to hurt Adena or the baby." Arashi snaps at Nathaniel.

Nathaniel and I froze in spot. We have not told everyone yet. I look at Arashi with my why did you say that look that didn't faze her one bit because she had no idea we didn't tell Bruce or Dante yet.

"What?" Arashi looks confused.

"Baby? What baby?" Bruce asks.

"Umm Bruce Nathaniel and I need to tell you something. We haven't actually had a chance to break the news yet with everything that's been going on." I start to explain.

"Okay. What's go on?" Bruce asks.

"Well." I looked over to Nathaniel for him to come stand next to me so that we can tell everyone together. He come to stand behind me and wraps his arms around me immediately clothing me in his protection and warmth. So here's go nothing. "I'm pregnant."

I expected for everyone to be a little bit of happy but the expressions on everyone face is surprise and worry. I look everyone in the eye one by one until my eyes landed on Quentin. I remembered his reaction to the news and immediately knew what everyone was thinking. They all think I'm going to die when I give birth to the baby.

Quentin must have seen the realization on my face so he tries to change the mood in the room. "Congratulations to you both." He says and even try's to throw in a supportive smile. Everyone looks at him like he's crazy and I know that I'm not about to get a congratulations from anyone else. I detach myself from Nathaniel and run up the stairs to my room shutting the door behind me.

I just want to lay down and not think about the outcome of me being pregnant but its impossible being connected to Nathaniel and hearing everything everyone is saying downstairs.

Nathaniel: "What the hell is wrong with you'll? It wouldn't bother you'll to act like your happy.
Dante: "But if she gives birth to that baby she's going to die like our parents did giving birth to us."
Nathaniel: "She's not dying."
Dante: "Come on Nathaniel you had to consider it."
Nathaniel: "No the hell I didn't because it's not happening. Adena is not going anywhere."
Arashi: "I'm with Nathaniel on this. Things have changed a lot over the years and we are not sure that our mothers die once they give birth to us. We still have a lot of research to do."
Bruce: "Yes Arashi we do. But because Adena is already pregnant we only have nine months to find something or someone who have survived giving birth.
Arashi: "Then let's get to it."

Quentin: "We have to find the rest of the scrolls in order to find new information that can get us those answers.
Bruce: "Yes the Scrolls. Let's get back to those."
Arashi: "What scrolls?"
Quentin: "Adena and I found a new scroll a few days ago. The day she pulled you to her. There are more but we have to find them. We think they are hidden within the other scrolls."
Arashi: "Okay so let's go check them out."
Nathaniel: "You need to boil some water. I'm going to check on Adena.
Arashi: "Boil some water?"
Nathaniel: "They will tell you."

I know Nathaniel is coming to make me feel better but I don't want to feel better. I want to know that my baby and I will be okay. How can I walk around happy about being pregnant when I will possibly be leaving my baby without a mother? What kind of life am I really giving my child? If it's a girl, she can never have kids unless she's ok with dying and not being there and if it's a boy, he possibly loses the love of his life to his child. How is that different from what Nathaniel is going thru with his dad now?

"Stop beating yourself up Adena. Everything will be ok." Nathaniel says. I didn't even hear him come in the room. My thoughts are nagging me and I can't help the way I feel.

"How can you be so optimistic Nathaniel? What if I do die?" I ask Nathaniel with my face pushed into the bed.

"Because I will never let you die and you will never let anything happen to you before knowing our baby is ok."

"As much as I would love to believe that Nathaniel, the truth is all of our mothers died giving birth to us. All of us. We can't just ignore it like it's not a possibility." I raise my head from the bed and turn to look at Nathaniel. His face is unwavering in his belief that he won't lose me. I wish I could feel the same.

"All I'm saying Adena is don't condemn yourself before knowing for sure. Yes our parents died giving birth to us. To twins. We don't know if we're having twins or if this connection we share changes our odds. Trust that our bond can overcome this before you accept death in the place of both our lives Adena. Trust that we are the exception to this so called curse everyone is trying to turn this into." Nathaniel says those words with pure confidence. His belief made me believe. Our connection gives me the strength and trust I need to see the possibilities in what he is saying. There is a lot to consider. This pregnancy may not be a death sentence but a new beginning.

"Did you practice that speech?" I ask smiling at Nathaniel.

"I don't need to practice. I'm a natural." Nathaniel says as he pulls me into him and comforts me.

"Yes you are." I only wish he could share the news with Joel. Maybe we can reach out to him. Just to let him know. Yea we can do that.

"Don't even think about it." Nathaniel protest.

"But I didn't say anything yet. I hate this connection." I pout.

"You love it." Nathaniel says with a little laughter in his voice.

"I think you should reach out. You two didn't leave on a good note this time Nathaniel. He may feel abandoned by the only family he has after all these years." I try pleading with Nathaniel. He's as stubborn as I am when I don't want to do something.

"Adena don't push this. If he wants to talk he knows where he can find me."

"But Nathaniel I think it'll be good for you both if you reach out to him."

"No. And that's it Adena." Nathaniel ends the conversation. As much as I want to let it go I don't think I should.

"Nathaniel he's your brother. You don't have to have that hardcore demeanor when it comes to him. He wants you to see him simply as your brother and not someone you need to protect or shield from pain. Give him his independence and let him be his own person. Not just your little brother." I'm determined to make my point. To get him to see that he needs his brother in his life just as much as I need Arashi in mine. Just as much as Joel needs to know who he is. But the only way he can find out is if Nathaniel lets him be independent and not just his little brother. "I'm not giving in on this Nathaniel."

"I see. You just used your words and your thoughts to attack me with your point." Nathaniel smiles.

"Sorry I just feel strongly about this."

"I know Adena. Just give me time. I need a little adjustment time myself too.

"Of course." I agree.

"Now are you going to take your own advice and talk to Arashi? Looks like she can use her sister right now. You both do." Nathaniel throws my own perspective back in my face.

"Yea, yea, yea."

"You ready to give them a hand looking through them scrolls." Nathaniel asks.

I take a deep breath before responding. "Yea. Let's go."

Everyone is working hard trying to find the other the scrolls but I can tell by their faces that they are not having any luck.

"What's wrong?" I ask.

"The steam isn't working." Quentin answer.

"Whatever you did Adena you need to try it again." Bruce says.

"I was angry the last time and then Quentin said something that stopped me. I don't know if I would be able to control it without burning the scrolls."

"Well what did you say to calm her down Quentin?" Arashi ask.

"Let's not recap." I intervene.

"Okay so we have to piss you off and then calm you down before you burn the scrolls. Should we just leave you and Quentin alone and let you recap and see if the same results happen again." Arashi tease.

"Not funny." I say to Arashi with a firm look on my face.

"There is another way to get Adena to let out steam without her getting angry." Nathaniel says.

"How?" Bruce asks.

"No." I say surprised from what Nathaniel is suggesting. "Nathaniel no."

"What?" Arashi ask.

"That could work too." Dante add.

"Am I missing something?" Arashi ask.

"Sex." Dante answer.

"Oh ok. Well go for it." Arashi say with humor in her voice.

"Are you insane? I'm not doing that with all of you looking at us." I snap.

"Why not? It's not like we won't hear you anyway." Arashi say.

"Adena calm down. We're not going to have sex. I can get you worked up without us doing that and don't worry they won't hear anything." Nathaniel smiles his cocky smile.

"That sucks." Arashi pouts with a roll of her eyes.

"Shut up Arashi." I say. "Nathaniel what are you talking about?" I ask.

"Just trust me." Nathaniel says.

He turns me until I'm facing him. He takes his time looking me over until he gets to my eyes and holds me in place with a strong look of desire in his eyes. I try fighting my arousal especially with everyone in the library staring at us but Nathaniel's look only turned me on. It felt something like the first time Nathaniel approached me here in my room. I couldn't deny him. I wanted him despite the feelings I had for Quentin at the time. Nothing else mattered. All I wanted was him at that particular time. Like all I want is him now.

"Don't Move." Nathaniel orders.

I don't know why but I don't move an inch. Not even when he walks away from me. I don't know what he's doing or where he goes but I don't care. I can still feel the desire of his eyes like they're still on me. Like he's still standing in front of me in need and want.

It's enough for me to forget that anyone else is in the room with us.

When Nathaniel makes it back in front of me it's like he never left. His eyes just seem a little more intense. I can feel the warmth from his body as he brings himself closer and closer to me. He stops so close to me that if I breathe I would accidently kiss him.

"Close your eyes Adena." Nathaniel says. This time I can hear the urgency in his need for me in his voice. Without hesitation I close my eyes.

I don't know what to expect. What will Nathaniel do? I don't think I care anymore about him doing it in front of everyone. My senses are heightened and my need for him is growing. The anticipation is killing me sexually.

I'm trying to take deep breaths in and out. In and out. In and out. I think I'm starting to take control of my myself again until suddenly the blackness behind my eyelids start to look like the bedroom in Nathaniel's place.

"How?" I start to say when Nathaniel puts his finger over my mouth to silence me. He takes his finger from my mouth and start to slowly drag it down my chest. He slid it down further until he reaches my belly button. I hold my breath thinking he's going to put his finger inside my belly button but his keep going down until he reaches the folds of my pussy.

That's when I realize it. I'm naked. Where did my clothes go? Before I can ask myself the twenty one questions that are sure to take my mind off what Nathaniel is doing to me, his finger enters me. I suck in the air around me and try to control the sudden shiver that comes over me. As I try to control this feeling, Nathaniel takes his thumb and start moving it in a circular motion on my clitoris. It sends an instant jolt through my body making me lift my hands to grab hold of Nathaniel.

"Put your hands down. Don't move." Nathaniel orders.

I do what I'm told but the feeling is starting to get overwhelming. Nathaniel starts to move both fingers at the same time. One going in and out. The other still making circles with my clitoris. Nathaniel fingers start moving faster and faster at the same tempo. I could barely stand.

I feel myself rising up on my tip toes trying to take control of this feeling but all it does is increase the tempo of Nathaniel's fingers inside of me. Suddenly I feel Nathaniel breath on my neck. His chin holding me in place by my shoulders. The more I try to push up on my toes the stronger Nathaniel hold with his chin gets. I'm so close. So close to exploding and the first thing that comes to mind is that everyone will hear. I start to panic and try to lift off of Nathaniel fingers without moving like he said.

"Oh no you don't." Nathaniel whisper to me and the next thing I feel is another finger entering my ass while his other two is sexually assaulting inside me and on my clitoris. All three fingers quickly bring me to my breaking point and I come hard and long. Nathaniel must know I can't stay quiet so he starts to kiss me. His kiss takes in every scream I'm trying to get out. He kisses me long, deep and passionate enough for me to come down from my orgasm without making a sound.

My legs are too weak to stand anymore so I fall forward into Nathaniel arms. Like always, Nathaniel catches me and make sure I'm okay. When I finally catch my breath I look up at Nathaniel and see this sort of proud look on his face.

"What the hell you do to her?" I hear Arashi ask.

"Helped her to release some steam." Nathaniel says without taking his eyes off me.

I quickly get myself together and stand back up on my own. Whatever Nathaniel did to clock our surroundings is gone now because we are surrounded in a room of steam.

"Wow. Did I do all of that?" I ask in amazement.

"Yes and it worked. Look, all the scrolls are coming apart now." Dante say.

I couldn't help the smile on my face when thinking about how I did it but my smile quickly goes away when I see the look on Quentin's face. He looks hurt and it sends a small feeling of regret through me. I feel my heart clutch a little for hurting him. I don't know what to say so I just say nothing and hid myself back in the comfort and support of Nathaniel's arms.

Chapter 16

We gather all the scrolls together. Separating the original ones from the hidden ones. Finally we are about to get some answers. Some answers that we all been looking for. The only problem is that Joel started this journey with us and he's not here to receive the information with us.

"Hey can we take a minute? I need to talk to Arashi." I ask.

"Sure. We can wait." Bruce says.

"Is everything ok?" Nathaniel asks me.

"Yes. Just taking you up on your advice." I answer.

"Now? You've been waiting for these answers for a long time Adena." Nathaniel says.

"A few more minutes wouldn't hurt anybody. Just make sure no one reads them without me." I say and kiss Nathaniel as I get up.

Nathaniel holds my hand a little longer trying to check and see if I am ok. To ensure him, I looked at him and smile, then walk away.

"What's up Adena? Is something wrong?" Arashi ask as we walk to the back of the safe house towards the forest.

"Yes. I just want to talk to you."

"Okay about what Adena?" Arashi's a little thrown off about my timing for wanting to talk to her.

"About Joel. I think he should be here with us when we read those scrolls. There might be valuable information for him in there too."

"Adena he chose where he wants to be and that's not here." I can hear the sadness in her voice. Like she's lost Joel and he's not coming back.

"No he didn't Arashi. He's simply trying to figure out who he is. You can understand that with all we been through. Not knowing is hard to accept. He finally found his real brother and wants to know more about him. There's nothing wrong with that. I think we should support him in his choice."

"What did you think I was doing Adena? Leaving my own life behind and following him wherever his leads took him. I did nothing but support him and it's like he forgot I was there when he found his brother."

"Arashi we both know that Joel loves you. He would have never let them hurt you or left you behind. He trusted that his brother wouldn't harm you. If he thought otherwise he would have tried to take them on all by himself. Don't let one misjudgment destroy the relationship you have." I plead for Arashi to hear me.

"I get what you're saying Adena. I don't believe that if he had a chose to come home with me or choose to stay with his brother that he will choose me."

"Well I disagree. You didn't see the look on his face when we left. He looked like his heart was being ripped from his chest."

"Really? Did it look anything like this unwanted fist print on my chest. That wasn't a love tap Adena. A simple push would have done.

"Arashi I don't think he meant to hurt you like that. It was as much as a surprise to him as it was to us when they merged together. He could have only wanted to put himself between you two but something else happened. You won't know unless you talk to him."

"Okay. When he calls I'll let you know." Arashi say.

"Arashi…"

"Adena I hear you but the reality is we don't have time to wait. We can't make everyone wait for our selfishness. We're not the only ones who need some answers Adena or are you pretending not see the hurt in Quentin eyes everyday just being here and watching you with someone else. I'm sure he would like to move on."

I didn't realize the pain I was putting Quentin in. I know it hasn't been easy for him and I shouldn't ignore that but I didn't ask him to come here.

"I'll see you back inside Adena. I'll let everyone know you'll be back in soon. Don't stay out here beating yourself up over this too long. Do you want me to send Nathaniel out here?"

Arashi waited for my response. It took me a minute but finally I said "No. I'll be in in a minute. Let me clear my head before I overload it with more information.

I smile so that Arashi can go back in without worrying. I know if she is unsure how I'm taking this she would send Nathaniel out in hopes of making me feel better.

"Okay." Arashi finally say and go back in the house.

I walk deeper into the forest to clear my head but I can't shake the thought that Joel should be here. Joel should be with us when we read the scrolls. The mood that Nathaniel and Arashi have been in the past few days is due to the absence of Joel in their life. I refuse to accept that they have moved on.

Without a thought I blink into the place I last knew Joel to be. As I suspected the room is filled with others like us again. They instantly surround me.

"I don't want to fight. I just want to talk with Luke." I say.

"Looks like you're going to have to settle with us." One of the guys says. When I look at the person who says it I notice him from the last time we were here. He's the one that absorbed Arashi hit. I guess I didn't think this all the way through.

I look around and notice the spot where Joel and Luke were standing the last time. It leads to somewhere else but I have to get up there to find out. I don't think I ever blinked from one spot to another when I wasn't fighting or looking for Nathaniel, but I guess now is a good time to try.

I blink out away from everyone and blink back in toward the opening where I saw Joel and Luke standing. Before anyone can catch on to what I'm doing I run full speed through the opening not knowing where I'm going. I should have bought myself some time, a few seconds at least.

As I'm running through this hall I notice all these different doors. What the hell Joel can be anywhere. I don't have time to look into every room so I call for him and hope he hears me.

"Joel." I scream as loud as I can. "Joel where are you? Joel."

"Looks like I'm going to have to take away your visiting pass." The same man from the last time says. Who is this dude?

"I'll just let myself in again."

"You're not getting away this time."

"We'll see." I smile.

He start walking towards me so I start walking backwards. Backwards until I ran into somebody. Holy shit. Nathaniel is so going to kick my ass for this. I turn around ready to fight. I'm about to hit whoever is behind me until I see Joel's face. I have to catch myself before I hit him so I throw myself back landing on the floor.

"Shit!" I yell.

"Adena what are you doing here?" Joel asks.

"I need to talk to you about Arashi and Nathaniel." I get up from the floor and rub my butt. I fell harder than I expected.

"What happened? Is Arashi ok?" Joel panic.

"Physically yes. Otherwise I'm not sure. Is there somewhere we can talk without the crowd behind us?"

"Umm yes. Its okay guys. I got her." He has to give them a stern look before they leave. It looks like they're not willing to leave me with him. I guess they don't trust him that much.

"Such a friendly bunch." I say being sarcastic.

"Yea. I know." Joel replied. "Adena what are you doing here? Is Arashi ok?"

"Yes she's fine Joel. Arashi, like the rest of us wants you to come back."

"Then why are you the only one here?"

"You know how stubborn Arashi and Nathaniel can be Joel."

"Yes I do."

"Then come back with me Joel. We found the missing scrolls that Sensei Arobi hid. We all should be together when we read it.

"Those scrolls were written for you and Arashi. They have nothing to do with me."

"They have information about all of us in general Joel. They could very well have information you may need as well."

"Adena I know you mean well. I just need more time to figure things out."

"To figure things out or hide away because you're hurt?"

"He had no right to keep this from me. Neither did you." Joel snaps.

"He was only trying to protect you. In his eyes he didn't want you to feel like he wasn't your brother and he didn't want to lose you." I try explaining how Nathaniel feels about the situation, but the look in Joel face is telling me that he doesn't really care. "Look

Joel there is something you need to know that I think is best coming from Nathaniel."

"What?"

"Come back with me so that Nathaniel can tell you." I plead.

"No Adena. I'm not coming back. If there is something I need to know then just tell me." Joel says. He looks at me with what looks like sadness in his eyes. I know he's looking for information but it doesn't look like he's happy with what he got.

"Arashi's been sad lately. She's been on edge a little without you. You have the same look on your face now." I try to get him to see he's not the only one hurting.

"I know. I did that. I do miss her Adena. I wish I could come back and pretend that everything is okay but I can't. I don't know who I am. All my life I've been Nathaniel's little brother just to find out he's not my real brother. Then the whole thing with our foster parents didn't help. You have no idea what he did to me. The worst part about it is that Nathaniel let him knowing that I wasn't his son. Knowing that we weren't really brothers. He took my choices away from me. How would you feel?"

"I would feel hurt, angry, disappointed and alone. Joel I get it. I understand why you feel the way you feel. It's okay to be angry. Just don't push us away. Don't hold it in. Face him and tell him how you feel. It's the only way you will be able to truly move on with or without him in your life." I tell Joel. He just stands there for a minute processing what I said. I can see him weighing the options in his head. He looks torn about coming back with me or staying here.

I don't say anything else I just let him sort out the thoughts in his head. I walk over to him to bring him ease. I slowly wrap my arms around him and wish I could make his pain go away. I wish that he will trust us and come back to us.

"It's okay. It's okay Joel." I say over and over. I start to feel him relax a little and his breathing goes back to normal. I'm about to say something but Joel's body gets stiff all of the sudden. Maybe he's just realizing I'm hugging him and is uncomfortable. I open my eyes and let go of him.

Something is off. When did we get outside? These trees look familiar. They look just like the one's…..."Oh no. I didn't. No!" I start panting. I can't believe I did this. Joel is going to be furious when he realizes I brought him back to the safe house.

"Adena is this where I think it is?" Joel asks me. I can see him getting angrier with each breath he takes.

I don't know what to say so I start to take steps back away from Joel. I can't believe I did this. I really didn't mean too. "Joel calm down. It was an accident. I didn't mean to bring us here. I was just thinking about being calm. I wasn't trying to leave or bring you here.

"Adena. Do. I. Look. Calm. To. You." Joel asks through tight furious teeth.

"Calm down Joel. I can take you back before anyone notices you are here." I say calmly despite the look of death Joel is giving me right now.

"Adena what's taking you so long? We're all waiting on you so we can read these… scrolls." Arashi stagger a little when she sees Joel. From the look on her face she's not sure what to say or how to react. "Joel." Arashi finally says.

Chapter 17

"**A**rashi I..." Joel starts to say something but doesn't finish. Instead he turns around and looks me in the eyes. "Take me back now!" Joel snaps at me.

"Nice to see you too." Arashi snaps back.

"Arashi I…I…" Joel stutters.

"You what Joel? Come on get it out." Arashi say. She looks at Joel with irritation showing clear on her face.

"I miss you." Joel finally says.

"That's why it took so long for you to come back? Or is that why you're in a hurry to leave again?" Arashi ask unwavering with her irritation.

"I don't expect you to understand what's going on with me Arashi. I didn't come here to make amends. I didn't ask to be here at all." Joel snaps.

"Then why are you here?" Arashi ask.

"Because your sister tricked me here." Joel looks back at me furious.

"I didn't trick you Joel. I was simply trying to be there for you and I must have blinked us to my safe zone. Where I go when I need to think and calm down. I didn't mean to bring you here. I don't exactly have my abilities under control with all the changes that's going on with Nathaniel and I." I try explaining.

"Well since you're here you might as well read the scrolls with us." Arashi say and walk back towards the safe house.

"I have nothing to do with that. Those scrolls include information about you not me." Joel says to Arashi's back as she walks away.

"If you care about me at all you will be there for me like I was there for you when finding your brother didn't benefit me either." She didn't turn around to face Joel. She just stopped her advances towards the safe house and waited for Joel response.

"Arashi if you want me here I will stay. But don't act like I dragged you along with me. You came on your own."

"Yes I did. I did because I love you. I did because I would have supported you with no questions asked and I trusted you. It didn't matter where you were going or why. I would have stuck by you no matter what Joel. You may not see it, but we are your family Joel. We don't need a damn blood test to confirm that. If you want to be here with us, then be here. If not then leave. Adena can't take you back though. She's kept us waiting long enough nagging us about you being here for this." Arashi says what she needs to say and goes back into the safe house.

Joel is standing here staring at the way back to the safe house. I know he wants to go in. I just don't understand what's holding him back. He can't be that angry over Nathaniel not telling him the truth. I got the feeling something else happened and he's having a hard time letting it go.

"Joel if you want to go. I'll take you back. I'm sure they will be okay waiting another minute." I say to break Joel out of this daze he is in.

"You made them wait long enough Adena. Let's just get this over with." Joel says and led the way back to the safe house.

"Okay." I smile and follow behind Joel.

We walk through the kitchen open doors of the safe house. Everyone has gathered in the living room with the scrolls lined up on the coffee table. When everyone turns around and sees Joel standing in the safe house silence fills the room. To say everyone is surprised to see him will be an understatement.

The silence doesn't last long thankfully. Dante and Bruce quickly get up to welcome Joel back with hugs. They tell him how good it is to have him back and start asking him questions about his long lost brother he found.

I'm happy for Joel to see that he is still wanted around. Even Arashi looks happy that he is here. She won't admit to it but I can see it on her face that she's happy to know Joel is ok.

Nathaniel on the other hand looks complex. He wants to be happy but he doesn't want to show weakness either. He just sits there with a blank facial expression on his face and watches everyone else interact with his brother. I walk over to him and sit on his lap. Nathaniel looks up at me and I can see the urge on his face to talk to Joel. He needs to know that they are ok. That Joel still sees him as his big brother.

"He does." I say to Nathaniel. Those two simple words are what he needs to hear. He takes a deep breath and pulls me into him.

"It's rude to listen in on other people thoughts." Nathaniel smiles up at me. I act surprise at his accusation and kiss him on the cheek.

"I don't need to listen in on your thoughts to know what's bothering you." I say and focus my attention back on everyone else.

"Okay. Okay. Okay." Let's get to these scrolls already." Arashi rolls her eyes at us and act irritated.

"Yes the scrolls." Bruce says. Everyone joins us around the table. We all take a deep breath hoping that these scrolls give us the information we are looking for.

I take a deep breath and pick up the first scroll to be read. Finally, we will get the information we have been searching for, for so long.

****

Scroll 1

Catrina Bushwarp	Randy Johnson
Maranda Kolster	Mary Cowheather
Micheal Randolph	Nathan McMacken
Christina Forthwright	Lori Evans
Claudette Wiggins	Claire Ford
Lucas Micheals	Antonio Blake
Linda Wright	Patricia Morgan
Rose Conway	Ashley Love
Brian Durham	Morgan Gaines
Maria Valenzuela	Rosalia Santana
Lina Gentry	Susan Barr
Herman Lozano	Steve Barron
Theresa Winters	Kate Forbes
Jaceb Monroe	David Gay
Taylor Hunt	Warren Boyd
Kelly Dunn	Valentina Velez
Lynn Best	Haley Meza
Duke Hatfield	Irwin Booker
Robert Brown	Jimmy Chavez
William Jones	Sean Ellis
Angel Lawson	Betty Johnston
Joseph Moore	Tony Wells
Edward Clark	Mike Porter
Matthew Allen	Glenn Wagner
Lacy Lynch	Ruth Carr
Leslie Richards	Carol Weber

Diane Andrews
Anthony Adams
George King
Kevin Green
Timothy Ramirez
Raymond Carter
Gabriel Morrison
Erika O'Brien
Paul Hamilton
Joshua Reyes
Jessica Jenson
Peter Ward
Victor Kelly
Craig Cole
Cecil Knight
Francine Frank
Samantha Lane
Jessie Simmons
Todd Fisher
Carl Flores
Aaron Sullivan
Wayne Rogers
Curtis Stone
Troy Black
Bernard Fox
Crystal Riley
Tonya Perkins
Candice Tran
Lia Watkins
Penny Austin
Joy Burke
Tracie Jacobs

Laura Sims
Melvin Palmer
Frederick Douglas
Chad Hicks
Jesus Chavez
Kyle Hunt
Sharon Knight
Michelle McCoy
Lee Dunn
Melvin Payne
Shirley Chen
Mario Woods
Vernon Stone
Hector Mills
Angela Reid
Melissa Hardin
Brenda Fields
Sam Schmidt
Alvin Rice
Corey Rose
Dustin Romero
Tyler Gordon
Jared Shaw
Neil Gibson
Ben Hawkins
Amy Walsh
Anna Little
Martha Fowler
Debra May
Amanda Bowman
Janet Day
Frances Newton

Lula Williams	*Teresa Lucas*
Rosie Hart	*Joyce Brewer*
Sally Queen	*Doris Holland*
Catherine Hansen	*Jean Banks*
Sanika Varcas	*Cheryl Santos*
Helen Chapman	*Joan Pearson*
Donna Lawrence	*Judith Barrett*
Lisa Lynch	*Janice Keller*
Sarah Oliver	*Judy Beck*
Beverly Bates	*Tammy Wade*

****

The names went on and on. Scroll one listed a bunch of names with no explanation of who or what these names were. Are they a list of people like us? If so, why are they grouped together? We know we are born in two's but none of these names matches the other.

Instead of trying to figure it out, I just look for familiar names. Like our names. If they are a list of people like us then our names should be listed.

"Well Adena, what is it? What does the scroll say?" Dante impatiently ask.

I take a minute to answer him in my hunt to find our names. When I look up at everyone staring at me so intensely I figure I need to tell them something. "It's a list of names. I think a list of people like us. I'm trying to see if I can find our names to confirm that but this list is so long. Why don't everyone gather around and look with me."

I place the scroll on the table so that everyone can see it. We all gather together to see if we can find our names on this long list.

****

Mark Vega	Richard Byrd
Jason Norris	Gary Craig
Adena Hartworth	**Arashi Powers**
Ronald Shelton	Paul Watts
Irene Byrd	Miranda Jones

****

I can't believe it. I found Arashi and I name. "Arashi look. I found our names."

"What? Where?" Arashi was practically on my back trying to see. I had to brace myself by putting my hands on the table to stop from hitting my chest on the table.

"Arashi you're about to smash me. Get off." I yell.

"Well, where are our names." Arashi urged. So I pointed to where our names are on the scroll.

"This can't be right. Why are our last names different?" Arashi point out. I didn't pay it much attention at first. I look at the scroll again and Arashi is right. Our last names are different.

"That is weird. Bruce do you know anything about this?" I ask Bruce since he is the only person Sensei Arobi ever trusted with anything about us.

Bruce mind starts to roam. I can tell he's thinking about old conversations he shared with Arobi about us. "If my memory serves me right, you and Arashi always shared the same last name. Even on your birth certificates."

Arobi must have changed our documents so that our last names will match. I'm sure if he did he would put some type of information in these scrolls so we can know why. "Let's not think too much about it. If Arobi changed our documents we should find out why in these scrolls. Let's just keep looking and see if we can find everyone else."

****

Cary Becker   Donald Franks

William Bolder   Harry Cole

Joe Mott   Jack Victor

Miranda Mory   Yolanda Morehouse

Justin Burke   Antonio McDonald

Nathaniel Stock   **Quentin Morrison**

****

Arashi jumps up all of the sudden surprising us all. We all just look at her trying to see what's wrong but all she does is hold her hands over her mouth. We wait and wait. Man, when is she's going to say something. The dramatics is starting to get irritating. Ok

I'm going to say something…. "Oh my God!" Arashi finally say.

"What?" We all practically say at the same time.

Arashi moves her hand off her mouth again and look up at Nathaniel. Nathaniel looks at me with the your sister is crazy look, so I roll my eyes and blow him a kiss before focusing back on Arashi.

"Nathaniel I found your name." Arashi puts the biggest smile on her face which throws all of us off because Arashi only does that smile when she's up to something.

Nathaniel rolls his eyes and shakes his head. I know he's trying not to let Arashi get to him but she already has. "Where?"

Arashi bounces up and down and point to where she found Nathaniel's name. We all follow her finger and the sound of surprises that come from our mouth is shock all over. Nathaniel grabs the scroll off the table to look at it closely. I can tell he can't believe his eyes. He looks up at me shaking his head. I can't even bring myself to say anything. My mind is going in multiple directions but one thing is clear. I feel sick.

I watch Nathaniel as he drops the scroll back on the table and leave. As much as I want to go after him, I can't. Before I know it I'm running. I run out the kitchen doors into the trees so that I can throw up. Nathaniel and Quentin are brothers? How can this be? Why didn't we see it sooner? I have to make sure Nathaniel is ok.

Walking back into the safe house I knew all eyes would be on me but I'm not prepared for the look on Quentin's face. The look of confusion, doubt, and then hurt as he looks at me. It's almost as if he blames me for the turn of events in his life. I open my mouth to say something but stop myself before words could come out. I don't know what to say. I don't know how to be there for him and Nathaniel without feeling like I'm choosing. Instead I go upstairs to check on Nathaniel.

Chapter 18

Nathaniel is sitting on the bed with his head pushed back against the headboard. His eyes are closed but I know he knows I'm here. I still don't know what to say so I just climb on the bed and lay my head on his chest. I feel the rise and fall of Nathaniel's chest as he takes a deep breath.

"Are you okay?" I silently ask. I figure that's a safe question to ask. It's a simple yes or no. Ok, it's not a simple question at all. How could it be? How can he go from not liking someone and almost killing him to finding out that he's his brother? What a stupid question.

Nathaniel interrupts my ongoing thoughts with his question. "Are you done debating with yourself about how I feel?"

"Sorry."

"I'm okay Adena. I knew I had another brother out there. I didn't expect it to be him. I been so blinded by everything else that I haven't took time to actually look at him. Maybe I would have seen it if I did."

"You can't blame yourself Nathaniel. This so called journey for answers has been hard on us all. If it wasn't for me, you and Quentin would have probably met on a friendlier occasion."

"Yea, I would have met my brother and his girlfriend and then ended up in this same position for stealing you away from him."

I couldn't help but laugh at what Nathaniel just said. It would have definitely been a struggle with us three. "Cocky much?"

"Adena we both know you would have given in to me sooner or later."

"You don't know that Nathaniel. The situation with Ren put us in a bad spot. It would have not been that easy if you would have met me while I was still head over hills for Quentin."

"Are you kidding me? Look at the connection we have Adena. Even if we didn't want to pursue each other, we would have ended up together anyway. We still would have hurt him."

Nathaniel is right. Our connection has been unavoidable since the first time we met. I can't imagine trying to fight it while still with Quentin. It would have hurt him too much. To finally meet his long lost brother and lose his girl to him. Both situations are bad.

We both lay with each other and just think. Our mind starts to entwine with each other, going back and forth, trading one thought for the other. Both our thoughts bring us to the same point. No matter what we both would bring Quentin pain.

Our thoughts had us lost in our conclusion that we didn't even realize that anyone else was in the room with us. "I know this must be hard for you to swallow but we need to get back to finding out what's in those scrolls. Everyone else needs answers too." Joel tone is mixed with concern but covered by anger.

Nathaniel raised his head to look at Joel. He doesn't say anything. He just looks at Joel with a passive look on his face trying to give the impression that he don't care. The silence last another thirty seconds before I can take it anymore. "We'll be right down Joel."

Joel looks at me and nods before leaving my room. I can't wait for them to make up. This tension has gone on long enough. "You think you can fix things with one brother before you worry about another?" I try to ask in a nonchalant kind of way but it comes out as irritated as I felt about it.

"You mind telling me how Joel got here in the first place?"

If I answer that question Nathaniel is going to be even more pissed. Instead I think I'll make my way back down with the others. I'll just answer his question on my way out the door. "Ummm…..NO."

Bad idea. I hear Nathaniel coming fast behind me. Thanks to this stupid connection I can feel how angry he is already. When I make

it back down stairs I sit between Bruce and
Dante. Nathaniel might not care about Dante
but he respects Bruce. To top it off I lean
back and rub my belly. It does what I expect it
to do. Calm Nathaniel down. When he sits
down on the couch watching me intently so I
can know it's not over yet, I smile at him. But
my smile soon falters when Quentin enters
the room. I gather myself and sit up.

"Did anyone find anything else in the
list of names?" I ask. I know they kept
looking while we were gone.

Of course Dante was the first to
speak. "I found my name. My brother name is
Ryuu Kuo. I wonder what he looks like."

Next was Joel. He spoke as if it didn't
matter. "I found me and Luke name too. We
need to keep going through these scrolls if we
hope to find anything else. I'll read scroll
two."

****

Scroll 2

*Merloni and I found as many people like
us as we can. We never directly introduced
ourselves so that we won't expose who she
was to the wrong person or expose them
to something they didn't know about. We
documented every name of everyone we
found. What we found was astonishing.
Everyone is born in two's with different*

last names. We learned that one child took the last name of the mother and the other took the last name of the father.
The oldest always took the name of the mother as remembrance of the mother after she passed. So Merloni and I documented the names in order of first born then put the second born next them.

We were hoping that in all of our research that we would find something new or someone who can explain to us more about this process. Why are they born in twos? Why must they have separate last names? Why do the mother's always give up their babies?

My questions are growing with more concern each day. Merloni seems to be content with the information she does have. I have not seen her worry yet. Even with the growing babies inside her. She kept saying she will never give her babies up. I know she never will but after researching into some of the others, they don't seem like the type of people who will give their babies up either. We just need to find out more. Our journey has only just started and it seems as if it's coming close to an end already.

I often fear something terrible is going to happen. I only hope it's something Merloni can survive. I also know that there is a great deal that Merloni is not telling me.

I have watched Merloni many times when she took her walks through the woods. I have seen her use abilities many times but never with me. She's afraid that with her pregnancy that she can hurt me if she loses control. But she never loses control.

I only hope one day she would trust me enough to show me.

We were fortunate to run into another person like Merloni. He was male and wasn't sure who he was. He used his abilities to steal from others. We ran into him as he was fleeing away from one of his victims. It was raining outside. The rain was coming down so hard you can barely see what's in front of you. He was headed right into us. I was about to move Merloni out of the way until her eyes start to change. It looked like a world wind swimming within her eyes. Without moving she froze everything around us. I saw the drops of rain all around me obeying her thoughts.

"You should watch where you going." She said to the confused guy clearly shocked by his surroundings. We both looked in amazement as the rain drops started to fall slowly to the ground. Merloni started a slow pace towards the guy. Although she had a smile on her face the guy was too scared to wait for her to get to him. With a blink of his eyes he was gone.

I didn't know what to think. I looked at Merloni as she turned and looked at something behind us. I turned to see what it was. It was the guy. He had somehow blinked away from us and looked as surprised as I was about it.

Suddenly I couldn't see him anymore because of the heavy fall of the rain again. I turned back towards Merloni and she had already started back walking.

This was the day I found out that Merloni could control things with her mind. I don't know what to call it or explain the changing of her eyes but it was one of the most beautiful and freighting things I ever saw.

We never seen that guy again, but I often hoped that he would find us.

After that day we looked harder for more information. The only thing we found out was that all the fathers seem to be human. None of them had abilities of any kind and none of them seem to be able to raise the kids on their own without the mother.

Merloni never told me who the father of her babies was or where she is from.

****

Joel squints his eyes at the scroll in confusion before looking up at us. "So who is Merloni? Maybe if we find her we can get some answers."

Arashi rolls her eyes at Joel as if he should know who it is. "Good luck with that." Arashi say.

"Why?" Joel asks confused.

"Joel she's our mom and she's dead." I answer.

Joel expression changes to sincerity. He looks over at Arashi with a sorry look on his face for not knowing. "I'm sorry. I didn't know. When did you find out?"

"Scroll four. It's the first scroll Adena found." Arashi response was empty. It's like she wants to say more but don't.

The silence is always awkward. There are too many emotions that need to be expressed between us all. But as always Dante is always willing to break the silence. "Should

I read the next one?" Dante ask with his finger raised in the air like a school boy.

Bruce passes the next scroll to Dante while we all watch. "I don't see why not." Bruce smiles one of his welcoming smiles. Bruce has always been able to make us all feel like one big happy family. I don't know where we all will be right now if it wasn't for Bruce.

Right on que Dante starts to read the third scroll.

****

Scroll 3

The hardest thing we had to realize was the new threat to Merloni. The mothers didn't leave their baby's; they died giving birth to the babies. Merloni is taking this information hard. She never thought that she would die. So our search for information continues. We decide to go to the United States. Merloni felt we could get more information from Chicago, IL. In our previous search we learned that there are a lot of people like Merloni living in this Chicago.

Our journey to Chicago was long. There was no time to really explore the city itself. Merloni wanted to get straight to finding out some information. We searched everywhere but everyone there was good at hiding and not willing to share any information they may know.

Merloni soon found out that the closer she was to someone like her she could feel their presence or the strength of their abilities. It helped us find them. A lot of them. But they all weren't happy to see us. Merloni start using her abilities on them to get them to talk to us. Soon she was known around for her ruthless acts of force to get information. When they saw her coming they either tried to fight her or just ran. Sometimes we learned nothing because they knew nothing of whom they were or where they came from. They were just trying to blend in before Merloni came along.

I feared that we had only wasted our time coming here. Until Merloni ran into another like her. This one knew exactly who and what he can do. He had full control over his ability. Merloni fought hard but could barely keep up with him. This guy moved like lightening. It was starting to look like this was a match that Merloni could not win. I watched as long as I could until I noticed that the guy was about to send a blow to Merloni stomach that the babies will not survive, so I silently moved in striking the guy with a blow to his chest sending him flying back. I turned to check on Merloni and she was in shock that I was able to do that. I might not have abilities but I am still a force to deal with.

As I reached for Merloni hand the guy grabbed me from behind, throwing me about ten feet away. I heard Merloni cry out before finally hitting the pavement. I jumped back up running to Merloni side but she was in no need of my assistance. Her eyes changed like before. She has completely taken control of his body. Merloni was about to go for the kill when her eyes suddenly turned fire red. She placed her hands on both sides of his head. Her head snapped back as her grip got tighter around his head. He started to scream from the pressure Merloni was putting on his head.

When Merloni head finally came back up and she opened her eyes, they were ice blue. Her touch now froze his head solid. Before she let go, she smashed his head into pieces. When Merloni came back to herself she passed out. I picked her up and carried her back to where we were staying.

Merloni slept for hours after that. After all this time of using her abilities she has never passed out before. It has to have something to do with the new abilities she used. I have never seen her eyes change three different colors before.

Almost two days had pasted before Merloni woke up. She was up bouncing around like it never happened. I told her what had happen and told her how long she was out. She couldn't believe it. She thought it was just a very detailed dream. Merloni said she have never experienced anything like that before. It was like something or someone took her over. The only explanation would be the babies growing inside her. As they grow, so does Merloni abilities. Merloni was happy to know that the babies had abilities while still in her stomach. I on the other hand was worried. What if their abilities are what kills her when she gives birth to them? The thought is too much to swallow.

Merloni never told me what she learned from the guy she killed. I didn't push for answers because she looked happy. She might have found a way to keep the babies and herself safe.

****

Dante smiles from to ear to ear had everyone staring at him. Was that it or is he just trying to torture us? "Your mom sounds hot." Dante finally say.

I roll my eyes and mumble idiot under my breath.

"What? I'm just saying she sounds like a badass." Dante grin would not leave his face. Like a little boy with a crush. He has a crush on my dead mom.

"Well this scroll told us something we already knew. Our mothers died giving birth to us." What Joel said is true. We do already know that but the realization really hit home for me. I might not survive giving birth to my babies.

My eyes lock in with Nathaniel's. I can see the anger in his eyes. The intensity of his eyebrows as they bunch up from the angry lines in his forehead. The fact that this may be the end for us is hard to swallow. The tears rolling down my face is for so many things. So many things I soon have to accept.

Arashi sudden loud intake of her breath brought me back to reality. When she spoke I barely hear the words that she says. "Adena, are you ok?"

I quickly wipe the tears from my eyes and put the happiest smile I can muster on my face before answering. "I'm fine. Don't worry about me."

"You're pregnant Adena. This can't be easy for you to hear." Arashi is right. It's not easy for me to hear but if we are ever going to find a way around it, I have to hear everything. I have to be prepared for what's to come.

"You're pregnant?" Joel asks surprised. That's when I realize we haven't told him yet. Nathaniel hasn't had the chance to tell him yet. Joel looks over to Nathaniel. Nathaniel try's to hide the emotions that are clear on his face from Joel. "I'm sorry." Joel says.

What anger Nathaniel was holding in came out. He stands up and walks over to Joel. He looks down at him until he locks eyes with Joel before saying something. "Keep your sorry. Nothing is happening to Adena. Nothing is happening to her or my baby."

Nathaniel looks around at everyone to make sure they all heard him. "Finish reading the scrolls without me."

"Nathaniel." I call out after him as he walks away.

"Here we go again." Dante say under his breath. I give him a cold look. Sometimes I just want to snap his neck. "I'm just saying. We're never going to finish these scrolls." Dante words manage to get him a cold stare from everyone.

I got up to go in search of Nathaniel. Before I leave I think it's best to let them keep reading the scrolls since it has information that everyone has been looking for. "Continue the scrolls without us. We'll read them later."

I don't give anyone time to stop me. I speed out of there so that I can be with Nathaniel. I find Nathaniel in one of my favorite spots. Up in the tress looking over the forest. I climb up and just stare out over the beauty of the view. I know Nathaniel will talk when he's ready. Besides we both need a mental break from everything.

"Nathaniel." We hear a call coming from below. It sounds like Joel. "Nathaniel." He calls again.

Nathaniel looks over to me for the longest seconds. I look back and forth in his eyes trying to figure out what's going on in his head. Nathaniel always blocks me out of his thoughts when he doesn't want me to know what's going on with him. I hate when he does that. He must have heard my thoughts because he smiles and then kisses me on my forehead.

"Nathaniel." Joel calls out again. After Nathaniel looks me over once more he jumps down out of the trees. I don't want to be rude and follow him so I guess I'll stay up here and listen from a distance. It is because of my efforts they're able to have that talk they need so much.

"Joel."

"Nathaniel. What were you doing up there?"

"Nothing. What's up?"

"Well honestly I don't know what to say. Congratulations I guess."

"Thanks Joel."

"Nathaniel I know you don't want to accept the fact that you may lose Adena with this pregnancy but you need to prepare yourself for that possibility just in case the answers you are looking for are not in those scrolls."

"Joel do you really think I haven't considered the fact that I may lose Adena? I have. I know that this pregnancy might kill her. I know that there is no known person who has survived giving birth to people like us, but I also know that Adena is different. I won't believe we were brought together to lose each other this soon. I don't believe everything is in those scrolls. Arobi himself said that Merloni kept things from him. There is a lot of information out there and most of it is locked in the mind of Adena's mom. We need to be out getting information from others like us instead of reading what we already know in those scrolls."

"Nathaniel if that's what you want to do, then do it. We'll do it together."

"You don't have to do that. I know you need your own answers."

"We're brothers Nathaniel. Saving Adena and taking care of my future nieces and nephews comes first. Before you say something else I'm not changing my mind on this.

"Thank you Joel, but even though I want to I'm not leaving Adena's side."

That's my Que. I jump down out the trees landing behind Nathaniel and Joel. There's no way they are going to look for information without me. "Then I'm coming with you."

Nathaniel turns around and gives me a stern look. "No you're not Adena."

I cross my arms ready to give Nathaniel hell if he thinks I'm going to sit here and wait for him like the last time. "Yes I am. Besides I'm the only one who can extract the information we need from them."

Joel laughs and throws his hands up looking at Nathaniel. "Don't kill me but she has a point. We can use her."

"We are not using the mother of my child for anything. She's going to stay here where she's safe."

"I will not Nathaniel. You can either take me with you or I'll go by myself."

"Adena don't try me." Nathaniel try's his stern tone on me, but he should know it won't work.

"Is that your final answer?" I ask ignoring the threat laced in his voice.

I can tell by Nathaniel's face expression that he's ready to pull his hair out of his head dealing with me, or better yet pull mine out. "Damn Adena! Why can't you just do what you're told?"

Now that made me laugh. "If I did that we wouldn't be together now."

"Now even I know that." Joel says laughing at Nathaniel and I back and forth bantering.

Nathaniel rolls his eyes at us and walks back to the safe house. "Let's just get back in there."

Chapter 19

There is intensity in the room when Joel, Nathaniel and I enter the safe house. Everyone looks worried except for Dante. He only looks worried that we will be mad about him continuing to read the scrolls without us. Everyone seems to relax a little more when they see the smile on Nathaniel and Joel face.

"So what scroll number are we on now?" I ask. I want to go searching for information with Nathaniel but I also want to finish reading the scrolls. They hold information about my mom. Someone I wished to meet my whole life but because of who we are, I couldn't.

"Scroll 5." Bruce answer. It's good we didn't miss anything. We already read scroll 4 so now everyone is caught up.

"So what are we waiting for? Who's reading scroll 5?" Nathaniel asks.

None of us were expecting who steps up next. It shouldn't be that much of a surprise. He has been with us here in the safe house researching for answers as well. "I will." Quentin says as he gets up to grab the scroll.

I can't take my eyes off of Quentin for some reason. He's been through so much and mainly because of me. I could have a least talked to him and seen how he was holding up. It's like I'm holding my breath for some reason until Quentin looks up at me. We hold each other's gaze until he drops his eyes back down to the scroll and take his seat.

****

Scroll 5

Merloni has been busy lately. The closer she gets to having the babies, the more she busies herself with preparations to leave them. She still hasn't told me anything about the information she has learned about people like her. She decided that looking for more of her kind is pointless now. She said she has all the information she needs.

We didn't go back home because Merloni wants to have the babies here surrounded by a city filled with people like her in it and she doesn't want me to be surrounded by a place in my own home where she dies.

Merloni doesn't think I know but she started her own journal. She locks herself in her room for hours at a time writing in it. I think she's writing to her babies so that they can have something to know her by. I also think she is writing what she have learned about who she is and who they will become so they won't have to search for information like we did.

I only wish that she trusted me enough to tell me. Lately our conversations have just been about her hopes and dreams for her babies. The things she wants them to have. The life she wish she could give them. The hope that they will find love without consequence.

I tried not to push Merloni for more information about herself. We have been great friends over these years and it saddens me that she will soon leave this world. I rather spend the time with her with a smile on her face then to see her sad from stories of her past and stories of a future she won't be a part of.

The days, weeks and months seem to speed past. Merloni stomach grows bigger and bigger. She comes to me with joy in her eyes. She tells me she knows what she wants to name her babies. The first will be named Adena Hartworth and the second will be named Arashi Powers. Those were the only names she gave me. When I asked her what if they are boys, she said that they are girls. When I asked her how does she know. She said she saw them with her own two eyes and they were two beautiful girls.

I didn't doubt her for a second. With as much I have seen over the years, I know that it's possible that she did see them. I just needed to know why the different last names. When I asked, she said that it is the way of her people. But I still could not understand why she would name one of her babies after a father who is not around. I didn't expect the laughter from Merloni when I asked.

She said "Arobi I have truly left you in the dark these past years. I did not mean to leave a bad taste in your mouth about the father. He was my one true love after all. If it wasn't for who I am, he would still be alive today. His name was Allen Powers. He was the kindest and most loving man I could have ever asked for. We were out on one of our dates to our favorite little place when we were attacked by someone like me. He was trying to rob us. He took Allen's wallet and jewelry. Allen told him that was it and to leave but the guy wanted more. He came for me to take the ring off my finger that Allen had given me. Allen jumped in front of me and tried to fight the guy off. The guy put his fist straight through Allen's chest. I felt as if he ripped through mine as well. It was the first time I used my abilities. I froze him in spot from the neck down. I wanted him to see me. To feel the pain he just caused me. I pushed my open hand through his chest slowly until I was able to grab hold of his heart. I wanted him to die a long slow death. I took control of the beating of his heart. Pumping it slow and hard. I can see the life slipping away in his eyes. I squeezed harder crushing his heart taking in the satisfaction that he can do nothing to stop me. I continued to squeeze until I saw nothing in his eyes. When he was gone I ripped his heart out of his chest and watched him drop to ground. I went to Allen afterwards and cried over him as he lay dead on the ground. I didn't think it would be possible to go on living without him after that happened. It wasn't until I found out I was pregnant that I wanted to live again. Live again to give birth to Allen's child."

Merloni story only made me want to fight harder to make sure her kids grow up to experience the type of love Merloni wants for them. I wish there was a way to save Merloni so her babies could know the wonderful mom I have had the pleasure of getting to know over these short years together.

Merloni asked me to take care of the girls for her. To raise them and teach them how to control their abilities. Merloni also wanted me to make sure they have a happy normal life. She said the time will come for them to learn who they are. She just didn't want them to be consumed with being different.

Merloni finally told me about the journal she's been writing. As I expected, she wrote down everything she have learned about who she is in that journal. She asked when the time is right for me to give the journal to the girls. She also asked me to keep researching in hopes that things will change for the best.

Her instructions were clear. Give the girls the journal when I feel they are ready to learn the truth about who they are. She said every question I have ever worried about and every question they will ever have will be answered in that journal.

I promised to protect her journal with my life and pass it on to the girls when they are ready.

****

My mom wrote a journal for us. A journal with all the answers to our questions in it. Well, where is it? Why didn't Sensei Arobi give it to us before he died? Why didn't he tell us this story before? Why did he want us to do all this damn searching for some scrolls with no information in it?

My thoughts are roaming angry in my mind. Question after question but still no answers. Instead of reading my mom journals with all the answers, we're stuck reading Arobi journals with no answers. It seems like we keep hitting these mysteries dead ends. Why?

I keep giving myself a mental beat down thinking about my mom's journals. Everyone is having a discussion about it but I'm too distracted to pay attention. I don't snap out of it until I feel Nathaniel hand on my shoulder. I'm so lost in my thoughts that I don't realize Arashi may be feeling the same. I look over to her and she's being comforted by Joel. He must've had to calm her down to.

I look over to Bruce. If Arobi would have mentioned a journal to anyone it would have been Bruce. "Bruce did Arobi mention a journal from my mom to you?" I ask almost in a panic.

Bruce thinks about it before responding. I know he wants to be sure but waiting is killing me. We have waited long enough. "No he didn't. But he did give me a bunch of books he asked me to keep safe for him. I just figured he really liked those books."

Arashi jumps up out of Joel arms and stand over Bruce in hopes that he will say that they are here with us. "So where are they Bruce?"

I can see Bruce sink into the couch. This can't be good. "I kind of buried them with Arobi."

Oh my God! I can't take no more. "Are you kidding me? I'll be dead by the time we get some damn information. I'm so tired of all this scripted shit. I'm starting to think the Japanese way is to irritate me to death."

I storm away from everyone and go to my room. Why does it have to be so damn hard to get a simple answer? Whatever we are, I don't care anymore.

"Adena?" Nathaniel calls my name not sure of how to treat me. I block him from my thoughts and I'm pretty sure my anger is resonating to an out of control level.

I look at him with blurred eyes. I'm not sure what I will do to him if he comes near me. "Nathaniel stays away from me. I can't be around anyone right now."

"I'm not going anywhere Adena. You can try your worst on me but I'm not leaving you.

I try to calm myself down so that I won't hurt Nathaniel but I can't. I been holding in too much and I'm finally at my breaking point. I'm about to give in to it until I hear Quentin voice. "Adena don't. Look at me."

I try focusing my sights on him but I can't. Everything is still in a blur. "It's ok." I hear him say. He's standing right in front of me. My eyes are a blur; it just looks like a wind world of clouds. I can't focus. I feel Quentin hands softly touch my cheek then slowly caress down my arms. "Let your mind follow my touch."

I do as he says and focus on his touch. I concentrate on every touch and feeling. He just takes his hands up and down from my shoulders down to the tips of my fingers. The feeling was almost like a divine distraction. A familiar warmth mixed in with a forbidden act. "That's it." Quentin whispers.

Before I know it I can see Quentin clearly. I can see the familiar look of love in his eyes when he use to caress me like this while looking out his window at the sunset. "Are you ok?" Quentin asks without breaking our eye contact.

I take a deep breath to think about my answer. There's nothing to really think about. I am ok. I'm just a little stunned that it's Quentin calming me down. "Yes. I'm ok." I finally say.

Quentin holds our gazes a little longer just to make sure. Then he walks away as if nothing happened.

Nathaniel blocks the exit for Quentin to get out. I can see he struggles with how to react. How to react to Quentin as his brother and not as his enemy. "What was that?" Nathaniel asks.

"Adena was about to blow. At the rate she was going she would have hurt us all. Since you two are connected, you being near her only would have increased the blow. I figured you wouldn't have minded if she blew me up instead."

Quentin push pass Nathaniel and leave. I can't believe he said that. Of course I would care. How could he think it wouldn't affect us if something happened to him? The situation between us three is ridiculous. We all need to talk and get whatever hurt or anger we feel for one another out so we can move on.

First I would have to survive the death stare Nathaniel is giving me right now. I know he's going to say something. I can see it on his face. He's mad about what just happened. Nathaniel opens his mouth to say something and I just freeze in spot. Okay here we go. "Are you ok?" Nathaniel asks.

I'm shocked. He's not mad. "Yes I'm ok." I finally say.

"Can I come near you now?"

I giggle because I did tell him don't come anywhere near me. "Of course Nathaniel."

Nathaniel practically rushes over to me. He hugs me with the tightest grip ever. "Natha……" I start to say but am cut short by his kiss. He kisses me hard and long. The passion he put in this one kiss is making my legs buckle. I throw my arms around his neck and wrap my legs around his waist. I want him right now. It feels likes forever since the last time we made love.

Nathaniel pushes me up against the wall and I feel the hardness of his cock pushing onto my vaginal. I rock up and down on him waiting for him to take me. Waiting for him to rip my clothes off and put it inside me. Nathaniel grabs my arms and pin them against the wall. The only thing I can think is yes. Take me. Take me now.

"Let's go back down with the others. They're worried about you."

I know Nathaniel can see the horror on my face from what he said. Is he crazy? I will blow up for real if he doesn't take me now. "Nathaniel no. I need you. Don't do this." I plead. I start rocking back and forth on his cock again harder this time. Nathaniel lowers he head unto my chest with a low moan. "Please Nathaniel." I whisper.

Nathaniel shakes his head no back and forth but I'm not giving in. I continue to rock back and forth on him. Causing myself to moan uncontrollably. I feel Nathaniel dick hardens even more. It's as solid as a rock.

When Nathaniel lifts his head and looks at me, his eyes are dark grey. I don't care. I keep rocking until Nathaniel throws me off him unto the bed. Without hesitation he rips my clothes off me. Leaving me panting on the bed. I silently wait for him to take his clothes off while struggling to control my own body. I can't keep still.

When Nathaniel drops the last of his clothes, he climbs on top of me. His self-control is starting to drive me crazy. I lift my legs to wrap around him and pull myself up to him. Nathaniel uses his palm to push me back down to the bed. He positions his dick at the entrance of my folds. On a deep breath he pushes in deep and hard. I scream out my satisfaction and want for more. I can feel Nathaniel dick pulsing inside me.

He lifts up and stares down at me while still deep inside of me, but I'm unable to stay still. I take control and push myself on and off him over and over. Nathaniel stays frozen in spot and let me work him. I close my eyes and grab my chest to try to control the sensitivity in them. But soon open them back up when Nathaniel thumb start to move in circles on my clitoris. I can feel my orgasm coming. I can't keep control of my legs anymore. Nathaniel has to hold me up because of my uncontrollable shaking.

It takes no time for me to cum. My orgasm comes hard. I scream out because of the intensity of it and because Nathaniel circles on my clitoris has yet to stop. It feels like my orgasm is never going to end. "NATHANIEL!" I scream out.

Nathaniel flips me over and starts to pound into me while holding both my wrist behind my back. The feeling is intoxicating. I can already feel another orgasm coming and Nathaniel have complete control over my body. I come again while Nathaniel pounds and pounds inside me. Then again and shortly after that again. My body is too stung by multiple orgasms to move. I feel Nathaniel pace increase as his orgasm comes to bay. I stay up long enough to feel him cum inside me. He finally lets my wrist go and we both fall limp onto the bed.

Chapter 20

When I wake the sky is dark and the moon shining bright. We were suppose to go back downstairs with everyone to finish reading the scrolls. I can only imagine what they must think. I know they must have heard everything.

Nathaniel is still sound to sleep. I don't think he rested like this in a long time. I don't want to wake him so I'll just throw something on and head downstairs. Hopefully they kept reading the scrolls without us. While everyone is sleep, I'll just catch myself up on what's in the rest of the scrolls.

I'm surprise to see Arashi down here just staring at one of the scrolls. She looks almost defeated by the information in it. "Arashi are you ok?"

"I can't stop reading this story about our dad. If this never would have happened we probably would have grown up knowing our dad. It's screwed up that this is our life. Instead of living happily ever after, we're stuck looking for answers to question I don't even care about knowing any more. I mean really Adena, what's the point?"

"I feel the same way Arashi. If it wasn't for me being pregnant I would just stop. In all this time our biggest threat out there was Ren. Now he just seems like a distant past to a blank future."

"We should be celebrating your pregnancy not worrying if you're going to die."

"I'm not going anywhere Arashi. I believe we would find out something. We haven't been searching long for information and based off the information in those scrolls, Sensei Arobi only knew as much as Merloni will tell him. The only information these scrolls gave us is information about our mother."

"Yea it did. I'm glad it did for us so we can know something about our parents. I don't know how that helps everyone else though. I feel like we're dragging them down a rabbit hole of our life."

Arashi words made me laugh even though they are true. It's like we're dragging them through the story of our life. "How about we finish reading the scrolls and give everyone the clip note version later?"

"Sounds good to me. I can't take anymore of you and Nathaniel distractions."

I slap Arashi's arm for teasing me about Nathaniel and I. Shaking my head I tell Arashi to read the next scroll.

****

Scroll 6

Merloni due date is close. Any day now she will be giving birth to two beautiful girls. For some reason I am as excited as she is to see these two new babies finally come to the world. The bad part is I will lose Merloni.

Merloni gave me a keepsake box she has been keeping since we have been here. She gave it to me to someday give to the girls. It holds all of her precious memories of her time with their father. She wanted them to know that he was a great guy. That they both would have loved them more than life if given the opportunity. Merloni and I often went to the store to stock up on the basic things the babies will need when they come out. Merloni also asked me to attend some mommy and me classes with her. She enjoyed the interaction with the other mothers and their babies. I use to think she asked me to go because she thought I would do a terrible job raising her girls, but that wasn't the case. Merloni didn't have a doubt in her mind that I would struggle with her girls. She just loved the feeling of being a parent despite her babies still being in her belly.

I can tell Merloni wasn't ready to let go yet. She's too young to die and no mother ever wants to leave their babies.

The next day I found Merloni staring out her window at the sky. I just watched her take in the everyday beauty of life. When she was done she faced me and said today is the day. I knew the day was coming soon. I'm still not ready to lose her. The day was coming to an end and nothing has yet to happen. I thought that maybe the babies weren't ready to come out yet. In a way I'm kind of happy to spend another day with Merloni. We have grown close over the years.

As the night creeps in, Merloni contractions grew stronger and stronger. I tried keeping her comfortable but the contractions were coming back to back. Soon her water burst and I knew it was time. Time for the babies to come out and time for Merloni to leave us.

As I stood waiting for the babies to come, Merloni and I locked gazes. Her eyes pleaded with me to take care of her girls and my eyes promised her I will.

Merloni pushed, surprising me with the amount of force she put behind it. That first push was enough for the first baby head to come out. I put my hands in position to grab the first baby. Merloni continued to push but I could tell she was getting weak. On her last push I pulled the first baby out and did all the necessary steps to ensure the baby was ok, in good health and safely detached her from Merloni. I wrapped Adena in a towel and took her to Merloni to meet her mother for the first time.

Merloni was weak but she mustard up the strength to hold Adena. She kissed her on the forehead, told her how beautiful she was and gave her back to me so I could but her safely in the bassinet while she push the second baby out. Merloni took a deep breath and pushed with everything she had. I can see the top of Arashi head almost out. Merloni pushed again and Arashi had come all the way out. Merloni fell limp. She was too weak to push again. I asked her to give me one last push and I'll do the rest. On another deep breath Merloni pushed with everything she had left. As I pulled Arashi out a bright ray of light filled the room. Merloni screamed out Allen's name right before passing out. The light blinded me for a moment and then slowly faded away. I hurried up to finish getting Arashi out so that Merloni can hold and kiss her like she did with Adena. Merloni was too weak to sit up so I helped her. Merloni smile was weak but she kissed Arashi on the forehead and mumbled the words beautiful before leaving us for good. I moved Arashi from Merloni arms and put her in the bassinet next to Adena.

I sat with Merloni for a moment mourning her. Merloni eyes suddenly opened and her body froze in spot. She looked straight up at the ceiling and said Allen it's too late. It's too late Allen. Then she was gone again. Till this day I don't know what she meant by that.

That day changed my life forever. I now have two babies to raise on my own. The next few days were a blur. I went through them doing everything Merloni and I discussed like a robot. I had her body shipped to me so that I can bury her where her daughters will always be with her. My journey back to Japan was a long one without her. If it wasn't for her girls looking just like her, I probably wouldn't know what to do with myself.

****

Tears are coming down both Arashi and I face. It's said to know that having us was the result of her death. The last name she called out was Allen's. Her one true love.

I look over to Arashi to make sure she's okay. She's taking the information hard. I go to her and hug her. "It's okay Arashi."

"It's not Adena. She really died right after giving birth to us. There's nothing in these scrolls that tells us of any other way to survive this. You're going to die if you give birth to those babies Adena."

"No I'm not Arashi. We talked about this. We will find a way."

"I know you want to be optimistic and all. But how could you after reading that. She was healthy and young. Nothing went wrong when she gave birth to us but she still died. Died right after."

"I have to be. You think I want to die leaving my baby without a mother? I know what kind of pain that will cause my child, you and Nathaniel. I need to be hopeful if we have any chance of getting through this."

"If you want us to get through it, then be realistic about what's going on. We need to be ready for what if. You need to start thinking about what if and so does Nathaniel. That baby will need him if something happens to you."

"I know Arashi. Just let me be optimistic for now. There are still a lot of things we don't know. Which mean there is still a possibility in my eyes."

Arashi looks me over before responding. She wants to believe there's another way but she can't see how. All things point to me dying during the birth of my child. "Ok Adena. I'll keep an open mind."

I smile at Arashi and grab another scroll. These scrolls are starting to way down on me emotionally. Six down. Seven more to go.

****

Scroll 7

Years have passed since I last wrote a scroll. The girls are now 3 years old. They're the happiest little girls I have ever seen. They carry their mother spirit in them. I see her in the both of them every day. They have been keeping me busy all these years.

I have time to write more now since my brother Bruce have been coming around and taking the girls for walks. He loves spending time with the girls. He treats them like little princesses all the time. It drives Ren crazy.

I haven't been keeping up research like I promised Merloni. It's hard when you have little ones to take care of. I can't bear leaving them without my protection. Over the past few weeks I have learned new things about the girls.

One night while they were sleep, Arashi had a bad dream. She was screaming at the top of her longs so I ran to make sure she was ok. I wasn't ready for what I walked in on. She was screaming and everywhere her little hands went the most beautiful blue ice flew from her hands. I didn't know what to do. I walked over to her dodging her little ice bolts. I don't want to know what will happen if one hit me.

I finally made it to Arashi and tried soothing her with a song. I sang an old Japanese song my mother use to sing to me. It calmed her down enough for me to pick her up. I rocked her back to sleep. She was sound to sleep when I put her back in her bed.

That was the first time Arashi had ever used her abilities. When I asked her how she slept the next morning she said fine as if it never happened. She was back bouncing and running around with Adena.

The first time Adena used her abilities was a scare. She and Arashi were outside playing like usual and Adena accidently dropped her Popsicle. She got so upset. I heard her scream from inside the dojo and ran out to them. When I made it to them Adena eyes were red all over. I can see steam moving from her body like a fire had just been put out.

I told her it was ok and we would get her another one. Her breathing was heavy. She huffed and puffed for a minute then eventually started to settle down. I watched as her eyes slowly turned back to their usual brown. She just looked at me and smiled and asked for another red one. I started to bring her a blue in hopes that it will cool her down but didn't want to risk her getting angry again.

Adena abilities had something to do with fire and Arashi's ice or water. It seems as if they only lose control over themselves when they are angry. Knowing that, I decided to start teaching them martial arts so that they can start to learn how to channel their anger into something more calming. To be so young, the girls caught on in no time. Even Ren was no match for them.

****

"Wow. We were bad asses at 3." Arashi say with way too much excitement.

"We were a danger to society. Good thing Sensei Arobi raised us somewhere where we couldn't accidently hurt anyone."

"Aww they would have been ok. As long as they didn't piss us off." Arashi laughs.

"Yea. Right." I rolled my eyes. We barely have control over our tempers now. Preschool would not have worked out so well for us.

"Are you ready to read the next scroll?" Arashi ask.

I'm starting to get tired again. As much as I would like to keep going the scrolls are like a rundown of our growing up. I think we can pretty much guess the rest. "Aren't you tired yet Arashi?"

"Hell no. I want to read some more about how bad ass we were.

"Fine." I grab scroll eight and just stare at it for a minute. At this point it's just another scroll to me.

****

Scroll 8

The girls are a little older now. They are eight years old now. They are into dolls and playing dress up. I had them their own little ninja suits made. They would jump, run and hide throughout the forest pretending to be real ninja's. Arashi really got a kick out of it. Adena would be in the mood sometimes and other times she would rather play with her dolls in her room.

I saw Arashi outside playing by herself one afternoon and asked her where was Adena. She said Adena didn't want to play today. I knew exactly where she was. She was in her room playing with her dolls. I asked her was everything ok. She smiled at me and said yes. She told me about her dolls and said she gave them all names. Adena only had one male doll so I asked her what was his name. She said Allen. I was surprised to hear that name again so I asked her why Allen. She said because lately she was having a dream about a man name Allen. I asked what type of dreams and she just shrugged her shoulders and said just dreams. I don't know what this mean. It could have something to do with their abilities. Maybe they have some type of connection with their parents. If so, why wouldn't she have dreamed about Merloni?

I left Adena alone to play with her dolls. Bruce stopped by to pay the girls a visit. I was happy to see him because I wanted to write about Adena's dream in the scroll. Maybe it will mean something when she gets older.

Adena reminds me of her mother a lot. She keeps to herself most of the time. Arashi is more of a free spirit. She must get that from her dad. Merloni use to tell me he brought the best out of her. I didn't know him but if he was anything like Arashi I can understand what Merloni meant. Arashi always brings out the kid in Adena. Sometimes I am afraid that Adena is growing up to fast. I can tell that she is starting to wonder about things. I only wish I could tell her about her mother. I don't want to see the sadness I will cause her when I tell her their mother died and how. Hopefully I have more time before they really start wanting answers about their parents.

****

"Weird much Adena?" Arashi tease.

"I know right. I don't even remember that. I don't even like dolls."

"Well apparently you did when we were 8 years old."

"I guess. I don't remember any dreams about a man name Allen either. You would think if I was having dreams about our dad I would remember."

"Maybe you didn't have a reason to Adena. We didn't exactly know anything about our parents back then. So the name meant nothing to you."

"I guess so. But Sensei Arobi is right. Why would I just dream about our father and not our mother? That's weird right?"

"I don't know Adena. Like you said, there's a lot we don't know about ourselves and what information our mother did leave for us is currently buried in a grave with Sensei Arobi."

I feel like we are on a never ending treasure hunt. The more information we find out, the more I realize we really know nothing. How many of us out there actually know something about who or what we are or where the hell we come from. So far it seems as if we are all in the dark. "Let's just read the next scroll." I pass Arashi scroll nine.

****

Scroll 9

The girls training have surpassed those of a master at such a young age. Soon, I will have nothing left to teach them. I can no longer hide information about their abilities from them anymore. They are learning more and more about themselves on their own and I think they are trying to hide it from me. I don't want them to think that something is wrong with them so I made the choice to tell them about their abilities. I will teach them to control them the best way I can although I have no idea how Merloni controlled hers. What I do know is that the girls only seem to lose control when they are angry. If I can teach them to control their anger, I think the rest will be easy.

I have to admit that this is more of a task for Bruce but I don't want to put him in an awkward position or risk him getting hurt by others because of this secret.

Adena and Arashi are becoming a threat for Ren. I can see that he's worried that their quick learning of my teachings will sway my decision on who will gain my title when the time is right. He knows there is no way he can beat them fighting. I worry when Ren starts to get creative. I raised them as a family but I am not blind to the distance protecting the girls has caused between Ren and I. Over the years I have written my intentions and plans for him within scrolls in case I don't get a chance to tell him myself.

It may be a few years before I write another scroll. Despite my promise to Merloni, I have not found out any new information for the girls. I refuse to leave them by themselves to search for answers to questions that have not been a threat for these girls. No one had come looking for them. From my experiences with them, their kind is not a threat. They are like us in many ways. The only thing that makes them different is their abilities.

****

Chapter 21

I can tell Sensei Arobi was struggling keeping up with these scrolls. Nothing about us was changing at the time and his concern was more so over Ren. I bet if he knew what Ren was actually thinking in his head he would flip out.

I want to finish reading the scrolls but I don't think they have any real answers to the questions we need answers to. What we really need to know is who we are and whether or not I'm going to die giving birth. It would also be nice to find out why?

I look over to Arashi to see if she wants to keep going. The long yarn she just made tells me she's just as tired as I am from reading these scrolls. "You want to stop for now Arashi?"

"No we can keep going. There's not many left to read anyway. I say we just get it over with. We've wasted enough of everyone's time."

"I wouldn't say that Arashi, but I get what you're saying." I do agree with Arashi that everyone must be tired of hearing the stories of us growing up. I also think that the information is helpful in some ways. We are all the same. It's possible that some of the information they have heard explains things that happened to them when they were growing up. But whatever. They should have the choice to read the scrolls or not. What we really need is the information in Merloni's, our mom, journal. That's what we should be concentrating on getting. The digging up of Arobi grave is a little disturbing though.

In the midst of my over thinking again. I hear Arashi clear her throat. She's ready to read the other scroll. Maybe I should have just stayed in bed with Nathaniel.

****

Scroll 10

Years have passed since I last wrote a scroll. The girls are now teenagers and turning into beautiful young ladies. I am no longer the protector of these girls. They have remarkably taking control over the protection of this Dojo. They said it is time for them to take care of me.

Ever since Ren left with his son Dante, I haven't been myself. After all my protection over the girls, I had forgotten that I need to protect Ren as well. I never thought that he would meet someone like them and fall in love. I have lived to long in this bubble, thinking that they will never need anything from the outside world. Although they spend a lot of time outside the dojo, I never imagined telling them about what else is out there. Ren's pain from his loss pushed me to start my research again. I asked Ren to talk to me about what happened, but his hate towards me is giving him pleasure knowing I want to know something he won't tell me. I know that the babies are born in twos, but Ren only brought home one baby all those years back. I can't help but wonder what happened to the other baby. I guess I should be glad the other baby is somewhere else so he wouldn't have to endure the anger Ren inflicts on Dante for the loss of his mother.

Since the girls are capable of taking care of themselves and the dojo on their own. I ask Bruce to come to the dojo for a couple days with the girls. I know the girls don't need him but his company is welcomed from the girls. Besides it will ease my mind while I'm gone to know the girls have someone here with them.

My journey started with finding information out about Ren's love. I wanted to know more about her and about him. How did they meet? Did he know about her abilities? If so, he must have known or figured out that Adena and Arashi was like her as well. I wish he would have come to me. I could have saved him from the heartbreak of her dying. I could have warned him.

My search leads me to her name. Her name was Kazumi Kou. As I expected she had no family. She had no real place she was living. People usually saw her when she came into town. I learned that Kazumi and Ren spent a lot of time together picnicking. Some say Ren use to bring her home with him. If so, I have failed as his father. I didn't even notice if Ren brought her to the dojo.

People who may have known Kazumi said she stayed to herself a lot. They were surprise to see her with Ren. She never really talked to the boys who approached her because she knew it was only for her beauty.

Ren would have been immune to her beauty growing up around Arashi and Adena. It would have given him the upper hand when meeting her.

She had to talk to someone. She couldn't have been here all by herself. Especially at such a young age. Whoever she was here with must have stayed to his or herself all these years as well. I had to find out who *she was here with. I believe, like Merloni, she would have stayed or trusted someone like me who would keep her safe and not ask a lot of question of who she was. Instead of asking random people about her, I decided to start visiting local Sensei's. They would have had to been near here for Kazumi and Ren to meet as often as they did.*

It took days for me to finally get to the last dojo. It wasn't as close as the others. It's almost like it was purposely built out this far. There are no students here. The dojo is still well taking care of. As I walked through the entrance of the dojo grounds I was greeted by who I assume is the Sensei here. The surprise look on his face tells me he doesn't get many visitors here.

He was still kind to welcome me in. I could have been an old man just looking for a short rest on my journey. I thanked him for his generosity. His name was Sensei Shou.

Shou asked me what I was doing traveling so far out. Instead of telling him a false story I told him I was looking for information about Kazumi. He showed no knowledge that he knew her but I know he does. I can see a secret hiding in his

eyes. Besides it's the same look I will give
if someone asked me about Merloni,
Adena or Arashi. I know it well.

Before Sensei Shou spoke, I told him who
I am and that I know about Kazumi and
my son Ren. I also told him I have too
kept a secret about someone like Kazumi.
I told him of Merloni. I didn't mention
Adena and Arashi to keep them safe.

Sensei Shou thought long and hard about
everything I told him. It was hard to tell if
he was considering believing me or
dealing with knowing there is others out
there. I told him I know the importance of
keeping their secret. I have kept Merloni's
long after her passing.

When Shou decided to talk to me about
Kazumi, I learned that Kazumi
experiences were much like Merloni's. She
too went searching for answers. But was
unable to find out as much as Merloni did
alone. At her age, I could only imagine the
struggles she had.

I asked him about the birth of Kazumi
and Ren's babies. I ask why there was
only one. From my learnings they were
always born in twos.

Sensei Shou said that Kazumi tried to hide the pregnancy from him but he already knew. He could start to see the changes it was having on her body. Kazumi tried staying out longer each day so that Shou wouldn't notice her. She left early to avoid Shou seeing her and came back late when she thought Shou was sleep.

On the night she gave birth, Shou said he heard noises that night. He knew something was wrong so he went to go see what was going on. When he walked into Kazumi room she was passed out and Ren was crying over her. When Ren saw him, he grabbed the baby and ran. Shou went to Kazumi to make sure she was ok. She wasn't. He thought she was dead until her eyes suddenly popped open. She screamed and pushed. That's when he noticed she was pushing out another baby. Shou said the baby came out in a ray of bright lights. He didn't know what would happen next. When he tried to go get the baby, Kazumi grabbed him by the arm and stared at him. He now realizes she was trying to gather enough energy to tell him something. All she managed to say was she was sorry. She passed out and that was the last time he saw her alive.

*I asked Shou what happened to the baby.
He said he has been raising him as his
son. He doesn't know about Kazumi or
Ren. I asked to meet him but Shou said he
doesn't think it would be a good idea. I
told I don't wish to introduce myself as his
grandfather. I would be okay with just
meeting him as a fellow Sensei and
knowing he is ok. Shou agreed even
though he really didn't want to.*

*His name was Ryuu Kuo. He was the
spitting image of my son Ren. As much as
I wanted to get to know him more, I
respected Shou wishes. Besides I don't
think Ren would be too happy about
another baby that took his love away.*

*The only thing that bothered me was why
Kazumi didn't tell Shou about the babies
if she knew giving birth to them would kill
her. When I asked Shou I saw the
disappointment on his face. He wasn't
disappointed with Kazumi. It was
something else. He told me neither him
nor her knew she would die giving birth to
her babies.*

*I can only imagine the devastation it
caused them all. I told Shou about Dante.
I didn't go in to much detail to spear him
more heartache. I know it would hurt him*

to think Kazumi's baby is not being well taking care of. I promised him that I will keep an eye on Dante as long as life will allow me. I hope one day that Dante and Ryuu will have the opportunity to meet one day. I know Dante will be excited to know something about where he came from and that it's not all bad. I only hope that I can get him away from Ren. One day Ren will regret how he treats Dante. Deep down I know he knows Kazumi would have wanted better for her son.

****

Arashi looks up at me with a surprise look on her face. We never knew Dante story and I know he would be happy to find out something about his mom.

"I can't believe Ren had a girlfriend. Someone actually liked him?" Arashi tease.

I couldn't help but laugh. I should have known Arashi was thinking something silly. "Really Arashi? Ren wasn't that bad."

"Whatever Adena. He was crazy back then. She must have been the only person he was ever nice too. He was like a bad version of Heath from Wuthering heights."

"How is that even possible Arashi?" I can't believe Arashi compared Ren to Wuthering Heights. She didn't even like the book enough to finish it. Maybe that's why she didn't finish it. It reminded her of Ren.

"What? Adena come on. Do you have a good memory of Ren at all from back then?"

"No. But that's because he was older than us. We didn't really pay attention or spend time with him back then."

"A good thing we didn't. He definitely would have pissed me off."

"Arashi you just like to find ways to fight. Hey we should sit this to the side for Dante. He'll be happy to know Arobi found his brother."

"Yea, he will." Arashi agree. She rolls the scroll up and set it on the side of her.

I grab the next scroll. At least they're starting to get interesting now. Maybe we will find out something else new. "Shall we keep going?"

"Only three left. It makes no sense to stop now."

****

Scroll 11

Sensei Shou and I decided to search for others like us who have helped people like Merloni and Kazumi. We started a Bond of Sensei's that protected and kept the secret of those like Merloni. We connected with shelters, churches and private government agencies to ensure the safety of the children born. We never told anyone of their abilities or differences. The only people who knew were those apart of the Bond of Sensei.

They may not know much about each other but they seem to find safety within dojos. In all, it gave us the opportunity to learn more so that we can pass the information. It helps those who came to us and helped us understand them more.

It's not many of us but at least those who find us won't have to die like Kazumi did without knowing.

****

****

Scroll 12

Bond of Sensei

Sensei Arobi
Sensei Shou
Sensei Hachiro
Sensei Isao
Sensei Jiro
Sensei Katsu
Sensei Ko
Sensei Masao
Sensei Shin
Sensei Tadao
Sensei Takashi
Sensei Takumi
Sensei Toshio
Sensei Tsuneo
Sensei Yasuo
Sensei Yori
Sensei Yoshi
Sensei Yoshiro

****

****

Scroll 13

Organizations

Hahaoya no ansen-sei
(Mother's safety)

Komyuniti herupu
(Community help)

Sensei Zaidan
(Sensei foundation)

Anzen'na hoko
(Safe directions)

****

The last two scrolls Sensei Arobi
wrote were lists of the Sensei's who help
others like us and a list of the organizations
we were able to go to for aid. I often
wondered what Sensei Arobi was doing when
he left the dojo. He spent his last years
creating these organizations for people like us.
I wonder why he just didn't tell us.

"Hey Adena do you think all these
Sensei's helped someone like us?"

"I believe so. I don't think Sensei Arobi would have told anyone who didn't already know about us."

"You're right. Sensei Arobi managed to keep it from us. I wonder if there is anyone out there that can tell us exactly what we are."

"You're not the only one Arashi. I just hope it's all worth it when we find out."

"I hope so too. Well since we finished the scrolls can we go to bed now?"

"Please!" Reading these scrolls made me sleepy. Arashi and I dragged our tired legs up the stairs and went back to bed.

Nathaniel is still sound asleep when I get back into bed. I would kiss him and lay down but I don't want to risk waking him up before I'm able to get some more sleep.

Chapter 22

I can't say I'm well rested. But it did feel good to sleep. As suspected Nathaniel is already up and down stairs. He's probably making his famous breakfast. I could use some food right now. I could also use a shower and a toothbrush. I can take a quick shower before Nathaniel brings breakfast up.

My shower takes longer than expected but who can get out of a shower when it feels this good. I better get out before Nathaniel comes up with breakfast. I want to eat that while it's still hot. Maybe I should surprise him and just go downstairs. Yea, I'll do that. I guess I better put a move on it than.

Finishing them scrolls took away some of the worry from me because I feel great right now. Instead of dragging down the stairs, I'm running this morning. It could also be because we are back together. Joel and Arashi are back and Nathaniel and Joel are talking again. What a relief

I'm just going to jump down the last few of these stairs for the hell of it. It makes me feel like a kid again. Now I just have to find Nathaniel. To my surprise, he's not in the kitchen cooking breakfast. He's on the couch talking to Joel. It must be a good talk with all the laughing they're doing. Although I'm happy to see them together again, I have to admit I'm kind of disappointed that there's no breakfast. Which is why I'm pouting when I sit on the couch next to Nathaniel.

"Morning." I say. I know my greeting is a little dry but I was really looking forward to that breakfast.

Nathaniel looks at me for a minute trying to figure out what's wrong. So I mustard up a fake smile for him. He smiles at me and shake his head like he knows what I'm doing. So I give him my 'what' face. I mean I am ok, I just wanted breakfast. Nathaniel and Joel continue their conversation they were having before I came down. I'm trying to pay attention to what they're talking about; I'm just not interested right now.

Forget it. I'm going to the kitchen to cook some breakfast. Why not? It is what I want.

"Adena." Nathaniel calls my name as I get up to go to the kitchen. I hesitate to turn around so that I can put my fake smile back on. "Your breakfast is on the stove."

My mood instantly changes. I take Nathaniel by surprise when I practically attack him and kiss him long and hard. I'm putting everything I got in this kiss so he can know how happy I am.

"What was that for?" Nathaniel asks.

"Just because you make me happy." I can't help myself. I kiss Nathaniel again before going to get my breakfast. My good mood is back and I'm about to finally eat the breakfast I've been craving for.

"Wow all that for breakfast. Maybe I should do the same for Arashi. Maybe it'll get her to at least talk to me." Joel interrupts.

I didn't expect that. Arashi didn't say anything last night about something being wrong with them. "What? I thought you two worked it out."

"Arashi is acting like everything is ok but she won't have a conversation with me about us. She wouldn't even sleep in her own bed last night."

"Well Joel. Maybe it's just the stress of everything. Finding these strolls, finding out about our mom and the journal she left us and me being pregnant has been hard for her to deal with as well. Maybe try talking to her about some of those things will help."

"Yea, maybe." Joel says. The look on his face tells me that he still think it's him that Arashi is mad at.

Well there's nothing we can do until Arashi tells us what's wrong and we can't do that until she gets up. Until then breakfast is still calling my name. Nathaniel left breakfast in the stove to keep it warm for me. I love that man. He always knows what I want.

The food smells great. It's my favorite. Pancakes, eggs, sausages, bacon and apple juice. Time to dig in.

Arashi finally comes down stairs and the first thing she does is take my bacon off my plate. I could kill her. "Good morning." Arashi dances away from me. She knows I'm going to get her for eating my food.

"Arashi stay away from my food."

"You don't even like bacon Adena. Why do you care if I take it?"

"I like Nathaniel's bacon. He knows how to make it. Unlike you." I give Arashi my stern look so she won't try to take anything else off my plate. She better make her own breakfast or put Joel to work.

"So when are we going to get the journal our mom left us." Arashi ask.

I lift my head to answer Arashi and notice that everyone has somehow gathered around and is looking at me for the same answer. Really? I can't finish my breakfast before we go into the never ending search for information again. I didn't mean to roll my eyes before dropping my fork back on my plate, but whatever.

"I was thinking maybe Nathaniel and I should just go since we can basically teleport there and back. Besides, I'm sure Sensei Arobi won't be too happy for us to be digging him back up anyway."

I didn't need a connection with Arashi to know that she is upset with my suggestion. "And what are the rest of us suppose to do while you and Nathaniel dig up our Sensei?" Arashi snaps at me.

"Everyone can take a break and catch up on a few things in the real world and get some things we need for the safe house. While you're out, can you and Joel grab some things for me and Nathaniel too?"

"Right because the rest of us are at your beck and call." Arashi snaps again.

"No you're not. What's up with you Arashi? Why are you upset? It was a suggestion so that everyone wouldn't have to go. If you want to go, then go."

"Fine. I think Dante should go to. He should check and see if his brother is still there."

"That's fine too Arashi." I don't know what's wrong with Arashi but she is being a bitch today. It's only been a couple hours since we last talked. What could have happened in that time?

"I don't mean to interrupt but I should go why?" Dante question made me realize we haven't told him about the scroll we read yet. Instead of explaining I go get the scroll and hand it to Dante. My breakfast is pretty much over, so I might as well clear my plate while Dante reads the scroll.

"He knew where my brother was all this time?" Dante asks.

"Apparently so. Arashi is right. You should go and see if he's still there."

"Good. Nathaniel can take Dante there while you and I go get our mother journal out of Arobi's grave." Arashi demands before walking away and going back upstairs.

I look over at Joel who have the I told you so look on his face. I still don't think her attitude is about him. Right now it's not clear what she is mad about. We'll figure that out when we come back.

"Let's get ready to go so we can get this over with. Meet back here in 15 minutes." I say. I walk pass Nathaniel and just shake my head. I want to go confront Arashi but it'll be better to just wait. Wait until we're alone so she won't have any excuses why she can't say what's wrong with her.

15 minutes past and we all meet back up in the living room. Arashi dressed in all black and mad at the world still, Dante with no real indication of how he feels, Nathaniel mad he has to chaperone Dante and not go with Arashi and I in case something happens and me. I'm irritated and ready to get back home already. Everyone else decides to go take care of a few things for themselves and for the safe house. I can't wait to get back to the bubble Nathaniel and I created at his

place. Hopefully nothing happens to prolong our trip while we are there.

I reach out for Nathaniel and Arashi hands prompting them to grab Dante hands so we can go. Without a word, I nod my head to them letting them know it's time. We blink out of the safe house and blink into the forest near Sensei Arobi grave. For some reason I feel uneasy like something is not right. Nathaniel must sense my worry because he squeezes my hand making me look up at him. His face is conflicted with the thoughts roaming through his and my head. The wrinkle in his forehead gets deeper the longer we stand here.

"Be safe." Nathaniel whispers in my ear before kissing my cheek.

"We will." I give Nathaniel a weak smile before him and Dante walk away. It feels weird now to be separated from Nathaniel. I feel like I need him. I know that's crazy but I can't ignore the feeling.

I watch them walk away until they are no longer in sight. Arashi is starting to get impatient.

"Can we get started now?" Arashi ask.

"Yea. Let's go."

The closer we get to Arobi grave the more I start to feel like something is wrong. Something I don't want to face but something I feel like I need to.

"You don't feel like something is wrong? Like we are walking into something?" I ask Arashi.

"Like what?"

"I don't know. Something"

"Adena is this some kind of weird thing you and Nathaniel have when you're not around each other."

I thought about that for a minute. Maybe it is. Especially with the pregnancy and all. "Maybe. I don't know."

"Let's just get this over with so you can get back to your love life and I can get back to my life."

"Don't you mean your love life? What's going on with you and Joel? Why are you being so crazy lately?"

"Nothing is going on between me and Joel. It's amazing how he can come back and start off where he left off with his brother and not make an effort to fix things with me."

"Wait I'm confused. Are you two not talking to each other at all? He thinks you're avoiding him and don't want him to come back. He thinks he messed up so bad you don't want him anymore."

"Stupid idiot. It's just a lot going on with all this crap trying to figure out who we are and all. Then on top of that you're pregnant and might die on me. I'm just dealing. Not avoiding him."

"Well you think you can tell him that. He really misses you Arashi and love you. Just talk to him."

"Okay. Don't nag me about it."

Finally Arashi and I are back to laughing and joking around. I miss us hanging out and being normal people. Before all the looking for answers came along.

We are getting close to Arobi grave. Finally we get to find out something about who we are from our mother. Maybe after this we can live out life as normal as can be. I can't wait to have a life with Nathaniel without us always worrying about each other. My badgering thoughts about it will have to wait though. There's someone standing over Sensei Arobi grave. A man. I never seen him before but he is one handsome man.

"Who are you?" Arashi ask the strange man.

"Just someone visiting a friend." He says.

"Arobi doesn't have many friends. If you are his friend, we've never seen you before." I say.

"I'm sure my relationship with Arobi was well before your time."

"That's weird seeing you don't look any older than we do."

"Looks can be deceiving."

"Apparently." Arashi say.

This man has a very strong presence. I can tell he's very confident but he also has a dark side he is trying to hide. He looks to be about six feet tall, with brown skin and bright green eyes. He has a Trey Songs kind of look.

Arashi suspension of people always put her in defense mode. Which is why I know that she is about to get ready to attack.

"Why are visiting his grave now?" I ask.

"He has been keeping something I hold dear. I needed it back."

That's when I noticed he's not just standing by Arobi grave; he's on top of it. Arobi grave looks fresh made. Oh no, Merloni's journal. "What did you take?" I snap.

"Why do you need to know?" He cocks his head to the side and look at us like he knows us. I don't know why or who he is but he's not leaving with that journal.

I look at Arashi to get her attention. When she finally looks at me I mouth the word journal and her eyes grow big with realization.

"Forget this." Arashi scream out. She attacks without a second thought. I follow right behind her. We both lunge in the air. Arashi feet first and me fist first. Right before we land our blows we freeze right in front of him. He just stands there looking at us for a minute. When he finally snaps out of it, he waves his hand sending us flying back into the forest. Arashi and I flip back landing on our feet. We look at each other with worry on our face. Neither one of us is strong enough to fight him and I'm pregnant.

I look up at him and slowly stand. I whisper "who are you?"

He turns his back to us. Without answering my question he walks away.

"Wait!" I scream and run after him.

"Adena don't." I hear Arashi say before she runs after me.

I blink out and blink in front of him. He's not startled or worried. He just stands there and stares at me. I look and see Arashi coming up from behind. She didn't have a chance. He froze her in spot before she could even get to him.

I don't think he wants to hurt us. He do want Merloni's journal just as much as we do so I just stand here. I watch him watch me. He just stares back at me.

"You look just like her." He says.

"Like who?"

"Like Merloni."

What? How does he...how does he know my mom. "How do you know her?"

"It doesn't matter anymore." He walks away from me to leave.

"Please. Who are you?" I wait for his answer. He stands with his back to me. He wants to tell me but something is holding him

back. He seems perplexed about it. "Please?"
I ask again.

Time seem to stand still waiting for his answer. He opens his mouth to say something but stops. Nathaniel blinks in next to me. He looks back and sees Arashi frozen and get ready to attack the man. I put myself in front of Nathaniel. "No!" I scream.

I turn my attention back to the man who has my mother's journal. He knows her. I don't know how. But he knows her. "Who are you?"

He turns around and looks at me. "My name is Allen. Allen Powers." He says and then he was gone.

"My dad…."

Meet the Author

Teresa Lucas

www.ingramcontent.com/pod-product-compliance
Lightning Source LLC
Chambersburg PA
CBHW070914180626
46817CB00003B/1059